TOTAL
COMMITMENT

Robert H. Austin

TOTAL COMMITMENT

iUniverse books may be ordered through booksellers or by contacting:

iUniverse
1663 Liberty Drive
Bloomington, IN 47403
www.iuniverse.com
844-349-9409

ISBN: 978-1-6632-1793-6 (sc)
ISBN: 978-1-6632-1794-3 (e)

Library of Congress Control Number: 2021902076

Print information available on the last page.

iUniverse rev. date: 02/18/2021

CHAPTER

Patsy Holt had spent over six years of her life traveling with her best friend, Middy Adams. Middy was one of the most successful cross- over singers in the history of country music. Her first five years had set new records in every field of music. She had won Entertainer of the Year for the past three years and had sold more recordings than anyone in recent history. She truly was a super star and super person to those who knew her.

Patsy had been the person to encourage Middy to sing. Without her support and encouragement, Middy Adams would never have been a singer; or super star…and they both knew it.

They had agreed to enter into Middy's career as a team, a true partnership. It had been that and more for over six years. They were together day and night. Middy's schedule was demanding and they seldom took time off. They both spent a few days with their families during the Christmas holidays and a few days scattered throughout the year. Middy went to Jackson, Tennessee to be with Tim and Mary, her adoptive parents and Patsy went to Austin, Texas with her parents. The rest of the time, it was concerts and the recording studio. Patsy was just as busy being Middy's manager, making arrangements for all of her appearances and interviews all over the country. Over a year ago, they had signed another five-year contract with RCA. Middy had insisted that Patsy's share would be forty percent of her total earnings. Patsy had objected, but Middy would not listen. She had reminded Patsy of their original agreement and the fact that she would not be a success without Patsy. So, it was done and they had been back on the road for over a year on their journey, together.

Patsy and Middy had become fast friends when they met at Kansas State University. They were roommates and both loved country music. After hearing Middy sing, Patsy knew she had talent and convinced her for them to move to Nashville, Tennessee and attend Vanderbilt University. She knew there was a good chance that she could be discovered and it had worked.

Patsy Holt loved Middy from the very first. She was so kind and seemed to be interested in her and her past. Patsy felt so close to her and enjoyed the time they shared in their first few weeks at Kansas State. Patsy wanted to tell Middy her secret, but was afraid of losing her as a friend. She had kept her secret inside her for all those years. Early in Middy's career the rumors started about them being gay lovers. Patsy could hardly discuss this with Middy. She knew Middy wasn't gay, but Patsy knew that she was. She wanted to share this with her best friend, but again, she couldn't bear the thought of losing her. She knew Middy came from a Christian family and wasn't sure if Middy would accept her if she knew her manager and best friend was gay.

Now, Patsy was thinking of taking time away from Middy. She was exhausted all the time and never seemed to relax. It made her feel guilty as she knew Middy had to be just as tired and exhausted as she was. She did think it must be some different for Middy though. Middy had the fans and the constant praise from every direction. Patsy was in the background for the most part. She did meet the stars and people Middy met, but she was just the manager. Middy always introduced her as her best friend and told everyone how she had been responsible for her success. But Patsy had to do something. She wanted to tell Middy her secret but needed some time to think. She wanted to ask for some time off and she felt she needed it. Not just to think, but to have some rest from the madding schedule. She decided to talk with Middy after the next concert.

CHAPTER

T hey had been on the road for three weeks when Patsy
decided to talk with Middy. They were sharing a room
in one of the finer hotels in downtown Dallas. The
concert had been sold out as usual, and they both sat and
looked at each other, as they sipped on a diet drink.

Middy smiled at Patsy and said, "Do you remember us
sitting in our apartment in Nashville sipping diet drinks
like this?"

"Sure, I do. That was the night we agreed to be partners,
right?"

Middy swallowed and said, "Yeah, that was the
beginning and it's been quite a ride. I hope you're still happy,
Patsy."

Patsy blushed as she thought about what she wanted to
say to her. "Middy, you know this has been a dream come
true for both of us, but…" She couldn't finish as she stared
at Middy.

Middy was shocked as she reached for Patsy's hand and
said, "Honey, is something wrong? I've never seen you look
so concerned, is it your family…your mom, your dad?"

"Oh, Middy, you always tell me I'm the worry wart and sound like your mother. Now, you sound like her."

"Well, I'm concerned. I'm so busy all the time, have I neglected something? Have I offended you?"

Patsy cried. She couldn't stand the thought of not being with Middy. They both sat in silence as Patsy sobbed softly. Middy held her hand and waited.

Patsy finally stopped crying, pulled away and got up and said, "I have to go to the bathroom."

Middy sat at the small table and waited for Patsy to return. It was several minutes before she came back and sat down.

Patsy looked into Middy's eyes and said, "I have a request and hope you will understand."

Middy's heart was pounding as she waited. "Patsy you know I'll understand, what is it?"

"I need some time off," she said without hesitation. "I'm just not feeling well and I think I need some rest." She hesitated again. "Please don't be mad at me. I can't stand it if you're mad at me."

Middy got up and walked around the table and stood over Patsy. She took both of Patsy's hands and pulled her up, facing her. They embraced in silence for a few seconds. Then Middy said, "Patsy, I don't have to tell you how much I love you. I would never want you to feel you couldn't take time off. I'm ashamed for being so demanding, I've been selfish and I'm sorry."

They stood back, holding hands. Patsy said, "I love you too. Are you sure it's okay for me to take some time off?"

"All the time you need," she said and kissed her on the

cheek. "I just want you to be happy, and well. Do you want to tell me anything else?"

Patsy was silent too long, then said, "I do, but not now, okay?"

Middy could only wonder what Patsy wanted tell her, and when.

They discussed the next concerts and agreed that Patsy would return to the tour in three weeks and hopefully have things back to normal. Patsy knew it would never be normal between them after she returned.

CHAPTER

Patsy was on a flight the next morning to Austin, Texas. She was going to surprise her parents and brother. It was only a one-hour flight from Dallas to Austin. She thought about her flight with Middy over six years ago when they had gone to tell her parents about their partnership. She remembered how supportive they had been and so happy for her. Now, she was returning home and not sure what she was going to tell her family when she arrived. As the plane descended, she thought about Middy and how shocked she looked when she told her she needed time off. She knew Middy was kind and understanding, but wasn't really sure she understood. She closed her eyes as she felt the plane touchdown and heard the sudden bump. She never loved flying and always said a silent prayer each time a plane landed. She rented a car and drove to her parent's ranch.

Her mom was in the kitchen when she walked in. They never locked doors as long as Patsy could remember. They had always felt safe living on a large ranch. The next ranch was over two miles away.

Sandy Holt ran to Patsy with open arms.

"Why, Patsy, what on earth are you doing here?"

"Hi, mom," she said as she hugged her.

Sandy frowned and took a step back. "What about Middy, is she with you?"

"No Mom. It's just me. I hope you are glad to see me."

"Honey, I'm always glad to see you, it's just a shock to see you walking in here."

"I know it is, Mom. I just needed to take some time off. Middy will be okay for a few weeks without me."

"You're not sick, are you?"

"No, I'm really fine, just a little tired from all the tours."

Patsy went to the fridge and got a diet drink and opened it. She thought about her and Middy drinking one the night before. She sat at the table and looked at her mom. She wanted to tell her what this was all about but knew she couldn't. She really had no one to talk with about her *secret*. She had read about people "coming out" and had seen several talk shows on TV regarding the subject. In most cases, these people had shown signs of relief and for the first time felt at ease with who they were. She was at that point now and needed to have that peace.

Sandy sat across from her daughter and said, "You look like you are in deep thought. Is there something you need to tell me, honey?"

There was that question again, her opportunity to tell someone. But, just like Middy, her mom was not that person. She smiled and said, "No, not really. I'm just glad to be home and looking forward to resting for a few days."

"Well, you came to the right place to rest and we'll see that you have all the rest you want and need." She looked at the kitchen clock and said, "Your Dad and your brother, Pete took a load of horses to the sale this morning. They should be back by suppertime. Let's not call them and let them be surprised like I was, okay?"

Patsy laughed and thought how much her family liked surprises and practical jokes. She knew her dad and brother would be totally shocked to see her.

"That sounds great; we'll surprise them for sure," Patsy agreed.

After the big surprise, the Holt family enjoyed a big supper and talked afterwards about a variety of subjects, none that could include what Patsy needed to talk about. She tried to join in with the laughter and fun but found herself becoming aloof and disinterested. Everyone noticed her lack of interest, but just thought it was because she was tired and needed some time to rest. The four Holts were in bed by 10:00 p.m. They were early risers and had always been. Patsy was ready for some early bedtimes. Her schedule for the past six years was never early to bed and for sure never early to rise.

Patsy had an old classmate from high school she hoped to locate the next day. They had discussed their sexual feelings and both had said they were interested in knowing more about homosexuality. That had only been a few times and it had been several years ago, but Agnes Barnes might be the one to talk with. Patsy would call her the next day. She fell asleep remembering their school days and Agnes' happy face.

CHAPTER

Her name was in the Austin phone directory, Agnes Barnes. She must still be single, Patsy thought. She called the number.

"Hello." Patsy did not recognize the voice.

"Is this Agnes Barnes?"

"Yes, this is Agnes Barnes, who is this?"

It did sound like her then. Patsy smiled and said, "It's Patsy Holt, how are you Agnes?"

"My Lord Patsy, I can't believe you are calling me, you're with that Middy Adams. Are you sure this is Patsy?"

"Well, it sure is. Do you remember who I went to the senior prom with?"

"Well, if this is Patsy, then you tell me who you went with."

"That ugly Steve T. Stewart, that's who,"

Agnes squealed. "You are Patsy. Oh, that Steve T. Stewart always used his middle initial like he was a big shot or something."

Patsy was laughing, thinking about her date with Steve T. Stewart. He had tried to kiss her, but she had resisted. He chewed tobacco and his breath was awful.

"So, where are you now, Patsy?"

"I'm home, here at the ranch." Patsy felt so good talking with Agnes. They had had some good times in high school, but had not seen each other since high school graduation.

"Oh, I would love to see you Patsy."

Patsy was so happy to hear her say that. "Well, that's why I called. Could we meet for dinner or something?"

"Oh, sure…when?"

Patsy didn't want to seem too anxious as she said, "Whenever you are available, I'm free for the next few days."

They agreed to meet at a local restaurant in Austin, that evening. They had gone there together when they were in high school. Patsy got there first and took a table near a window so she could watch for Agnes. She saw her getting out of her car and notice that she had gained some weight. She wasn't fat but was a full-figured gal now. Patsy, on the other hand had kept her schoolgirl figure, maybe some smaller now than when they graduated.

Agnes saw Patsy as she entered, then walked very quickly toward her. Patsy stood up and they embraced.

"You look so good." Patsy said.

"I'm fat; you're the one that looks good. Why, you look like you did when we graduated from high school?" Agnes blushed, showing her embarrassment.

"Well, first of all, you're not fat. I'm too skinny and I know it." She didn't want to embarrass Agnes.

They ordered and then sat and looked at each other before Patsy finally said, "So, I assume you haven't married by still having your maiden name."

Agnes looked embarrassed again. She looked away then back at Patsy. "I really haven't tried to find anyone, how about you?"

"The same, I guess. I've been on the road with Middy for over six years and just…"

She really didn't know what to say about not being married. She wanted to broach the subject they had discussed years ago but wasn't sure just how to say it.

Agnes made it easy for her when she blurted out, "I guess a lot of people think the ones of us who aren't married must be gay."

Before Patsy could respond, the server brought their salads and set them down on the table. Patsy stared at her salad and said nothing.

"I was just kidding, Patsy. Don't look so serious."

It was serious to Patsy. It was so close to the subject, but she was still afraid to address it.

"So, tell me what's like on the road with Middy Adams," Agnes said as she took a mouth full of salad.

"It's impossible to describe. The fans, the excitement, it's like a fairy tale or a dream."

"And, I'm sure you love it."

"Yes, I do love it, but I do get tired."

"You seem tired now, Patsy." She stopped then said, "I'm sorry, I don't mean that you look bad…me and my big mouth."

"That's okay. You're right though. I am tired and that's why I came home for a while."

Patsy wanted to know more about her old friend as she asked, "Well, you know what I've been doing. What about you, Agnes?"

"Oh, nothing exciting like you, Patsy." She blushed again before saying, "I work in a small animal clinic and assist the veterinarian. She's been really good to me and wanted me to go to veterinarian school, but I never will. I'm happy doing what I do and you know how much I always loved animals when we were growing up."

Patsy smiled as she remembered how she and Agnes used to visit the local vet together and check out all the little puppies and kittens. It was a different vet than her dad used. Their vet came to the ranch and only worked with large animals.

"I do remember, Agnes. I'm sure you must have a pet or two now."

Agnes laughed and said, "Well, not a pet or two, I actually have five cats and two dogs." She paused then said, "They're my family."

Patsy looked directly into her eyes and asked, "So, you have no one in your life?"

"No, just my cats and two ugly dogs, but they are all sweet and I love them."

Patsy loved talking with her. She was so funny and down-to-earth. It was great to be with her again after all those years.

They finished their meal and talked more about old times when they were in school. Patsy ordered a glass of wine and Agnes had a beer. She said beer was her friend and her hips and belly had to pay the price. They both laughed.

After the second round of drinks, Patsy felt she could explore the subject with Agnes.

"Agnes, do you remember us talking about gay people… years ago?"

Agnes took a big gulp of her beer. She drank from the bottle and never used a glass.

"Why, I do, but…

Patsy knew what Agnes must be thinking about the rumors about her and Middy. She had to stifle that. "Agnes, I'm sure you have heard the rumors about Middy and me."

Agnes smiled and said, "Well, that's none of my business, or anyone else's."

"As Middy and I have told the press and everyone else, it's not true. If it was true we would admit it." Patsy waited then said, "That's what I want to talk about."

Agnes looked puzzled as she said, "Talk about what, you and Middy Adams?"

"No, Agnes, I want to talk about what we talked about years ago, we both were interested in the subject of homosexuality, as I recall."

Agnes again looked embarrassed. She turned and signaled for the server. "I want another beer, what about you, Patsy, more wine?"

It was their third drink and they were both feeling the effects.

"Oh, Agnes, this is hard for me." She paused and then said, "I need to talk with someone about my sexuality."

"Is this why you wanted to see me, Patsy?" She took another gulp of beer.

"Yes. I want to let someone know how I feel. Someone that will understand and I think you will... am I right?"

Agnes leaned over and with a whisper asked, "Are you telling me that you're gay?"

Patsy couldn't speak as tears rolled down her face. She nodded and reached across the table and took Agnes' hand.

After a long moment of silence Agnes said, "I have never talked to anyone either. I'm so glad you called me today."

Patsy Holt loved Middy Adams, but she didn't love her

sexually. She wanted someone she could be with sexually and be in love with. She hoped this meeting with Agnes Barnes would be the beginning of her new life. She was afraid but wanted to find out if this was what she really needed to give her the peace she had longed for. She thought of the people she had heard about and read about…they had all said they were happy with themselves and had found peace after "coming out."

CHAPTER

Middy had never performed without Patsy being in the wings or somewhere in the same building. Now she was on stage trying to sing above her screaming fans. As she looked out over the sea of waving arms keeping rhythm to her song, she wondered what Patsy was doing. She missed her so much. She missed their talks after each show, the downtime, as she called it. It was a time to reflect and relax. She was always keyed up after each show and talking with Patsy was comforting for her. Now, she had to sit alone after the show, looking at an empty chair, wishing Patsy was in it. She hadn't called her, but was tempted to every night, just to hear her voice.

It had been three weeks since Patsy left and Middy decided to call her. They had talked about her taking three weeks. If Patsy needed more time, it was okay with Middy, but she did feel that Patsy should call her, and she hadn't.

Patsy's cell phone went directly to voice mail, "Hello, you have reached Patsy; please leave your message at the beep." It was her same greeting. Middy left a message and waited. Patsy always called back within minutes, but this time she didn't.

Patsy listened to Middy's message. It was brief. She had

said she hoped she was okay and would like to hear from her and to return her call, please.

Agnes came in from her bathroom and said, "Was that your cell or mine?"

Patsy was happy staying with Agnes, but now felt guilty. It was like her mom had caught her doing something wrong. But it wasn't her mom, it was Middy Adams. She felt that she had betrayed Middy as she looked at Agnes and thought about what they were doing. Then, she thought about how Middy had answered the reporters about the rumors. Surely Middy would understand. Middy wanted her to be happy and being with Agnes was making her happy.

It was two hours later when Middy's cell buzzed. She saw that it was Patsy. "Hello there, gal."

It was good to hear Middy's voice. Patsy was choked up and sounded like someone with a cold. "It's me, Middy. How are you?"

"I'm fine, are you okay? You sound like you have a cold."

"No, I'm just glad to hear your voice." She sobbed.

Middy was worried that she might really be sick. "Honey, you're scaring me, are you okay?"

"Yes Middy. I am just overcome. I miss you so much…"

"Well, you know that I miss you. It's so lonely every night after the show. When are you coming back?"

Patsy looked at Agnes. She was smiling and looking excited, knowing Patsy was talking with Middy Adams. "I'm not sure, but I do need to talk with you. Where is the tour now?"

"We just finished tonight in Houston and now have a few days off. I'm sure you don't remember." Middy paused.

"I am flying back to Nashville in the morning, could you meet me at home?"

Patsy wanted to see Middy as much as Middy wanted to see her, but there was Agnes. It was time, time for Patsy Holt to tell her best and closest friend her secret. She didn't answer Middy as she was thinking.

"Patsy, are you still there?"

Patsy's heart raced as she answered, "Oh, yeah. I was just thinking, Middy."

"Thinking?"

"Middy, I have an old friend from high school and I want to bring her with me. Would that be all right with you?"

Middy couldn't imagine why but said, "Well, sure. That's fine with me. Will you and your friend be here tomorrow?"

"We will catch the first flight out in the morning…and Middy"

"What?"

"I'm so glad to be coming back home."

Middy smiled and said, "Me too, see you tomorrow."

Patsy ended the call and looked at Agnes and thought she could finally tell Middy her secret and hopefully be at peace with her life.

CHAPTER

Middy and Patsy had purchased a home on five acres in the Franklin, Tennessee area. They had moved in just after Middy's first recording and it was obvious, they were going to make it in the country music business.

Many country music entertainers had located in that area. It was private and most homes were gated with some having security twenty-four hours a day. Middy and Patsy's home had a guard on the gate.

They really didn't like having the tight security, but without it, the fans would invade their privacy.

Middy had been home for three hours when Patsy and Agnes arrived. Agnes was mesmerized by the security and the size and beauty of the home. She stood in the large foyer and looked at the staircase. It reminded her of the set in Gone with the Wind movie. She turned to Patsy and said, "Good Lord, Patsy. I can't believe I'm here. This place is unreal, you must love living in a house like this."

Patsy smiled and said, "Well, it has its moments, but I never felt comfortable living here."

Agnes frowned and continued to gawk at her surroundings.

Patsy took Agnes by the arm and said, "My room is

on this floor, just to the left. We also have a guest room on this floor. It is just across from my room. I really need a few minutes with Middy."

Agnes knew Patsy had to explain their relationship with Middy. Patsy took her to the guest room and promised to return and take her to meet Middy.

Middy's room was the only bedroom on the second floor. The upstairs was designed for one person. It was complete with a full bath within the bedroom area. Other rooms on the second floor included a library and a small kitchen. Middy would not have designed this herself, but it was available when they were house hunting, so she bought it.

Most of the time Middy and Patsy were alone. They did have a maid and a cleaning lady. The maid was there mostly when they had guest. The cleaning lady came in once a week. Today, there were only three people in the house.

Patsy was more nervous than she could remember as she walked up the stairs and knocked on Middy's door. She had never waited for Middy to answer her knock; it was just a way to let her know she was there.

Middy met her in the middle of the room and hugged her. They had never been separated for more than a week since their partnership started. Their embrace lasted for a long time as they both cried.

When they finally stood back, holding hands, Middy said, "Patsy, I have missed you so much. Please don't ever leave me for so long again."

Patsy was speechless as she looked into the eyes of her best friend. They shared a love that no one could understand.

. Patsy thought of the rumors and how so many people still believed that they were gay lovers. Now, at this moment,

Patsy felt so confused. Her love for Middy Adams was the only love she had known, but it wasn't complete. That was what she had to try to explain as she continued to look deeply into Middy's pretty blue eyes.

"Well, are you going to stay home with me?" Middy asked. She couldn't understand Patsy's silence but felt that something was different.

"Middy, I'm back and I do want to stay with you, but..." She couldn't go on. She turned her back to Middy, covered her face with both hands and sobbed.

Middy placed her hand on her back and said, "What is it, Patsy? Are you sick? Please talk to me. I'm so worried about you, honey."

Patsy turned back to face her and said, "No, I'm not sick, but what I need to tell you makes me feel sick."

Middy was silent. She wondered what could possibly be so upsetting to Patsy. Then she thought about Patsy's friend. Her friend she had brought with her. "Patsy, is your friend involved in this?"

It was now or never for Patsy. She had to acknowledge the truth. "Yes, Agnes Barnes is the reason I need to talk with you."

Middy's first thought was that Patsy's friend might be wanting a job or money, some kind of special favor. "Does your friend Agnes want something from you? If she does, what is it? What could she want that seems to upset you so?"

"She wants me, Middy."

"What do you mean, she wants you?"

"Oh, Middy, I told you I wanted to tell you something when I left. Do you remember?"

"Yes, and I have wondered what it could be since you

left. We have never had secrets since we met. Please tell me, I love you."

Patsy felt almost faint as she said, "Middy, I'm gay."

Middy had wondered if Patsy could be gay when they first met, but after a few days, dismissed the thought. Now, it seemed that her first instinct had been correct. She controlled her expression and appeared not to be shocked by Patsy's confession. She cleared her throat and said, "So, it's Agnes and you? You and Agnes are lovers?"

"Middy, I can't stand it if you hate me. I love you and I need you in my life." She hesitated then continued. "I don't expect you to understand my sexual feelings. I have known since I was a teenager that I was gay. I wanted it to go away and not be true, but I can't make it go away."

Middy was a lot more shocked than she let it show. She wasn't sure how to handle the discussion with Patsy, but didn't want to say anything that would destroy their relationship. She again took Patsy in her arms and said, "First of all, I will always love you, Patsy Holt. It's true, I cannot understand your sexual feelings, but you of all people, know how I feel about gay people. I have no ill feelings about them. We have both said we would admit we were gay, if we were and I truly meant that." She waited for Patsy to respond.

"So," Patsy said. 'Are you telling me that you accept me, knowing who I really am?"

"Patsy, I'm telling you that I do accept who you are. It must have been very hard for you all of these years, living with your secret. How about your parents, other relatives and friends, do any of them know?"

"They will know now. I felt that I must tell you first. I

hope you believe me when I say you are the most important person in my life."

"I know and do believe you Patsy. You are the most important person in my life also. Now, we will have to make some living arrangements for you and Agnes."

Patsy knew that she and Middy would stay together, but still felt guilty. Middy had tried to make her feel at ease with her decision, but it would take some time to adjust. It was time to introduce Middy to her lover, Agnes Barnes.

Middy was gracious to Agnes and made her feel welcome in their home. Middy was never one to avoid the subject at hand. She smiled after being introduced and said, "Agnes, Patsy has told me about your relationship and I am fine with it. If you're okay staying here, I would love to have you live here with us…you and Patsy."

CHAPTER

Middy Adams, Patsy Holt and Agnes Barnes had now been living in the same house for three months. Patsy and Agnes shared Patsy's room and were both happy with their new lives. During Middy's tours, Agnes stayed at home and managed the household. She made sure the cleaning lady kept everything in order and was there when Middy and Patsy returned from each tour. It seemed to be a good arrangement for the three ladies.

Agnes had gone back to Austin a few days after they arrived in Franklin to place her pets in foster homes. Her friend and former boss had kept her pets at the clinic while she had gone to meet Middy with Patsy. Agnes knew a lot of people who had kept cats and dogs to keep them from being sent to the pounds where they were eventually euthanized. She was hopeful that she would be able to have them again, but knew that Middy did not like pets and would not allow them to be in their house. She hoped privately that she and Patsy could live somewhere away from Middy.

Middy was beginning to feel the loss of Patsy even though they were together on tour. Patsy was always on her cell phone to Agnes after each concert and talked less and less with Middy after the shows. Middy had become accustom to having that private time with Patsy, but now it seemed to Middy that Patsy was more interested in talking with Agnes, her lover.

They had been on tour for a week and Middy was sitting in the hotel room with Patsy, listening to her talk with Agnes. They would be returning home the next morning. When she ended the call Middy said, "Patsy, I want to talk with you and I want you to listen."

Patsy knew how they had always agreed to hear each other completely before speaking. This had been a rule Middy's parents had observed and Middy and Patsy had also made it a rule in their relationship. She listened.

"First of all, I'm not sure you are as committed as you used to be."

Patsy opened her mouth to speak as Middy stared at her. She closed her mouth and frowned.

"Okay," Middy continued. "I know you and Agnes are lovers, but we have a relationship also. I need your involvement and support, but I don't feel I have it. When we're on the road, its work… it's our job."

Patsy couldn't remember Middy looking sterner than she did at that moment. She wanted to comment but knew better. She continued to listen.

Middy did continue. "Patsy, you know how serious this business is. I'm not going to always be on top. You are not just my best friend, you are my manager and right now, I don't feel like I have a manager."

Patsy frowned a long time before speaking. Then she finally said, "Middy, I'm very disappointed by your comments." She stopped and wiped a tear from the corner of her left eye. "You know how much I love you, Middy. You and your career are my life, and I have given you my total commitment."

Middy smiled at her best friend and said, "Patsy we're not talking about our love for each other here. We are talking about business and your lack of interest lately."

"So, you think I've lost interest in our business arrangement, our partnership?"

"That's exactly what I think, Patsy. Now, I want to tell you why, okay?"

"I'd like to know why."

"Well, it's pretty obvious to me…it's your lover, Patsy."

"She has a name, Middy. You don't have to call her my lover."

"Okay, I deserve that. I should say Agnes; I know her name and as I have told you, her sexual orientation, and yours, do not bother me."

"So, what does bother you, Middy? Are you jealous of my relationship with Agnes?"

Middy waited before speaking. Now it was her tears that came. Middy shook her head and let out a long sigh. "Yes, damn it."

Patsy took her in her arms as she had done so many times when Middy was upset. They held each other for several seconds; neither spoke.

Middy was afraid that she was losing Patsy forever. She had tried to accept and understand their relationship, but really could not. She had nothing against gay people, but this was Patsy, the most important person in her life. How could she live without her?

Patsy was also thinking and beginning to think Middy was never going to accept her relationship with Agnes.

After a long embrace, they stood back from each other, holding hands. They were both crying. Both knowing this could destroy their partnership, their love for each other.

Patsy finally broke the silence. "Middy, what are you thinking? Are you saying you can't live with this arrangement any longer?"

It was hard for Middy to speak as she closed her eyes and said in a very soft whisper, "Yes, this breaks my heart, Patsy." She opened her eyes and looked into Patsy's eyes and continued. "Honey, I've never loved anyone like I love you. You have made me who I am and I will always be grateful to you for that. I just cannot go on living with this. When we get home, I want you and Agnes to find a place and move out."

Patsy stood with her mouth open as Middy left the room and went into the bedroom.

CHAPTER

T heir flight arrived in Nashville the next morning and
they were home in Franklin by ten.

Agnes was waiting for Patsy in their room. She could
tell by Patsy's expression that something was different.
"Well, you look like you just lost your best friend. Did you
and Middy have a fight?"

Patsy frowned and said, "Agnes, Middy Adams and I
have never had a fight. I've told you about our special love
we have. I know you don't understand it. It's not the kind
of love we have for each other. Middy and I have nothing
sexual about our love."

Agnes was frowning also. "Patsy, what are you saying.
Has she convinced you to leave me? I know she hates me."

"Agnes, Middy has never hated anyone including you.
She is not happy with our relationship and you know
that."

Agnes rolled her eyes and said, "How well I know. So,
what is this all about?"

"She wants us to move." Patsy could not say any more.
She covered her face and cried.

Agnes was happy, but didn't want to show how pleased she was. "Well, if that is what she wants, I guess we should move, right?"

Patsy looked back at her. "Yes, and I think the sooner the better for her and us."

CHAPTER

Middy Adams was alone in her multi-million-dollar house. She and Patsy had been together since Middy's career had started and now, she was alone with no one to love and no one to love her. Patsy had moved out and was living with Agnes in a Condo in Nashville. Middy could not stand the thought of living with Patsy and her lover under the same roof. So, it had been her decision to have Patsy and her lover to move out. Patsy didn't want to leave, but Middy had been very strong about her leaving, with her lover, Agnes Barnes.

Patsy had been heart-broken but thought her life should be with Agnes. They had been gone for three months and Middy and Patsy were still missing each other and both felt they always would.

Middy was envious of Agnes and envious of Patsy having someone to love and spend her life with. She was beginning to hate the road and her concerts. It wasn't the same without Patsy and her encouragement after each concert. She had sat alone in her room or tour bus and cried after each appearance. She needed someone but had no idea who. Then one evening after she had completed a three-week tour, she thought about Rick Stone. She sat and smiled, thinking how sweet he had been and how he had tried to get her to have dinner with him. She wasn't interested at the time. She was too busy with her studies and her friendship with Patsy. The last time she saw him she was too busy with her career and she still had Patsy. Now, she was so sad and unhappy. She wanted to call Rick, but what would he think? He could be married again and maybe be happy with a family. Then she remembered her dad always telling her to wait when she wasn't sure about something. She went to bed that night and dreamed about Rick.

The next morning, she called her agent and told her that she was taking a month off. Her agent was surprised and asked if she was sick. Middy had thought, "Yes, I'm sick, but not physically." She told her agent she just needed some time to rest and that she was okay.

Later that morning she called the Vital Statistics Office in Topeka, Kansas. She asked for Rick Stone and was transferred to Rick's secretary. She was a different one than Middy had met in Rick's office. She sounded professional and more intelligent. "Rick Stone's office, this is Kathy Crane."

Middy paused, not wanting to use her name if she didn't have to. "May I speak to Mr. Stone, please?"

Then came the obvious, "May I tell Mr. Stone who is calling?"

Middy tried once more, "I'm an old friend of Rick's. I'm sure he will take my call."

Middy waited as she heard the secretary exhale in the phone. "I'm sorry ma'am. I must have a name, please."

She knew it was going to be the only way to talk with Rick. "Tell him it's Middy Adams, I'm sure he will take my call."

Her voice was raised a level or two as she said, "I've heard Mr. Stone talk about meeting you…please hold on, uh…Middy…Adams."

Middy smiled, knowing how excited Kathy was talking to a country music singer.

He sounded the same and it warmed her heart to hear his voice after so long. "Middy, is this you? Are you all right? Oh, I can't believe I'm actually talking with you again."

Middy wasn't sure which question to answer first. "Yes, yes to all your questions. How are you, Rick?"

"Middy, please hold on for just a moment. I have some people in here and I need to excuse them."

"Oh, I'm sorry. I can call back if you are busy, or in a meeting."

"No, the meeting is being adjourned as we speak."

Middy laughed as she thought about Rick pushing his people out of the office.

He was back in a moment and smiling as he picked up the phone. "Now, we have a lot of catching up, Middy."

Middy thought how right he was, but wasn't sure how to start. She needed to see him in person, but first, must find out if he is still single. "Well Rick, have you finally found that special someone?"

Rick was smiling from ear to ear. "Yes, to answer your question. In fact, we're engaged and plan to marry next month."

Middy sat down hard in her chair. She had not wanted to hear this and it made it difficult to continue her conversation. "Well, I'm glad for you." She paused then said without thinking, "I guess I waited too long."

Rick was silent for a moment, and then said, "Boy, I wished you really meant that Middy."

Middy laughed softly and tried to gather her thoughts. "I've thought about you a lot lately, Rick." She really wanted to see him even though it was too late. She had to give it a try. "Rick, I'm going to Kansas in a day or so. I go there to visit my mother's grave and haven't been there for a while." She couldn't go on and paused.

"Wow, is it close to Topeka? Maybe we could meet."

That was all she needed as she said, "I would love to see you Rick."

Rick was so excited he could hardly think of what to say next. Then he finally said, "Boy, I've told Jenny about knowing you ever since we met, now she will actually get to meet you, Middy."

"Jenny is your girlfriend?"

Rick was quick to correct her. "No, she's my fiancée, my wife-to-be."

Middy wanted to spend some time alone with Rick, but with this comment from him it wasn't going to be easy. She had to think of something. "Rick, I'd love to meet your Jenny, but I really need to see you alone." She hesitated then said, "I could meet her during my visit, after we have some time to catch up on our past. Would that be okay with you?"

Rick wasn't too happy about meeting her alone but didn't want to say anything to spoil her visit, or maybe cancel it. "Oh sure, Middy, that sounds fine. Where do you want to meet?"

Middy felt like she was back in control and smiled. "I have rented a private jet for my trip and could pick you up at the Topeka airport, say tomorrow afternoon?"

Again, Rick was surprised with her answer. "Where would we be going?"

"I want you to visit my mother's grave with me. I can explain more when we meet. Can you meet me tomorrow at the airport?"

He didn't want to say anything to cause her to not see him. The next day would be Saturday and he was starting a week's vacation. A week to be with Jenny, but he couldn't resist the opportunity to see Middy. "Yes, what time do you want me there?"

"We will arrive around two tomorrow at the private terminal. I'm sure you know where that is."

"Yes, I've flown out of there a few times on private planes. I'll be there at two." He thought about Jenny and their dinner date for that night, but was sure he would be back in time, so he didn't feel he had to tell Jenny at this point. He could tell her all about his short visit with Middy during their dinner. He smiled and thought how everything would work out fine. Jenny had planned a day of shopping with one of her girlfriends and wouldn't expect to hear from him until their dinner date at seven on Saturday. His smile grew larger as he heard Middy speaking again.

"Thanks, Rick. I can't wait to see you again."

They ended the call. Middy was happier than she had been in months. Rick, on the other hand, was confused and a little concerned. Why did she want to see him alone? She had never indicated any kind of interest in him. He looked at the phone and again, thought of Jenny. He really needed to tell her but couldn't bring himself to call her. He thought again how he could tell her at dinner.

CHAPTER

At two that Saturday afternoon, Rick stood in the private terminal and watched as a white Lear Jet taxied toward the terminal. His mind raced as he thought about seeing Middy Adams again, but still had no idea why she wanted this visit to not include Jenny. He tried to put Jenny out of his thoughts as the jet came to a stop near the entrance. He saw the door open and to his surprise, a pilot came down the steps alone. There was no sign of Middy. Maybe this wasn't her plane.

The pilot entered the terminal and looked around and spotted Rick

. "Are you Rick Stone?" He asked.

Rick looked back at the plane and then at the pilot. "Yes, I'm Rick Stone."

The pilot extended his hand and said, "I'm Paul Watson, one of the pilots for Miss Middy Adams. She is waiting for you on the plane." He paused then said, "Do you need anything before you board?"

Rick released his hand and said, "No, I guess not." He followed the pilot into the Lear Jet.

Middy was sitting in the cabin with a broad smile as Rick entered. She was dressed in a white cotton shirt and blue jeans. After the pilot passed her and went to the cockpit, she stood up and opened her arms. Their embrace was long and tight. She whispered into Rick's ear. "I've been thinking about you so much and am so happy to see you."

Before they could continue their conversation, the pilot asked them to take their seats and secure their seat belts.

They sat facing each other and smiled in silence as the jet took off into the west and then slowly banked around toward the east, gaining altitude.

After they had leveled off Rick spoke. "Well, this is a real surprise to say the least, Middy."

"A happy surprise, I hope."

It all felt so strange to Rick. Here he was with the most popular country singer in a private jet flying somewhere... to see her mother's grave?

"Well, it is a happy time for me. Seeing you again is wonderful." He looked out the window and then said, "Where is your mother buried? You said in Kansas, I believe."

"Yes, she is buried in a small town not far from here. It's Junction City. Have you heard of it?"

"Yeah, I know most of the towns in Kansas, but have never been there. So, we should be there soon?"

Middy smiled and said, "Well not now, I want to show you my place first.

Rick couldn't think of anything to say except, "Oh, that sounds nice."

"We're only a little over an hour to Nashville, then a thirty-minute drive to Franklin."

"You live in Franklin? Is that part of Nashville?"

Middy smiled. She knew this was a strange thing to do to someone. "No, it's south of Nashville and much smaller."

Middy offered Rick a drink from the bar on the plane, but he declined. She wasn't sure if he drank alcohol and didn't ask. They both had a diet drink and talked about the first time they met.

Rick wanted to ask more about why she wanted to see him alone but remained quiet about it. He couldn't stop thinking about Jenny and what he was going to tell her. They had planned to have dinner and now he was flying in a private jet, going to Music City, USA. Would he get back in time for their planned dinner?

The flight was like Middy had said, only a little over an hour. Now they were in a white limo driving south on I65, heading to Franklin, Tennessee. During the last hour and a half, Rick had kept his eyes on Middy, admiring her good looks, but feeling guilty about his bride-to-be back in Topeka. He had wanted Middy from the first time they met when she was trying to find her biological father. He had never been in love with her, but had dreamed of being with her, and yes, even being her husband.

Rick felt the soft touch on his arm and came back to the present. "Rick, you seem to be in deep thought." She squeezed has arm. "I know this is a strange thing to do, but I hope to put your mind at ease when we get to my home."

Rick again decided to wait as she had asked. "I'm fine Middy and I am looking forward to seeing where you live."

They rode in silence until they arrived at Middy's home. It was more than he had expected. However, he had never been in an entertainer's home before. He stood in the large foyer and gawked. Middy knew he was amazed and allowed him to take it all in. She finally touched his arm and said, "It's too much isn't it?"

Rick wasn't sure how to answer so he just smiled and continued to look around. He pointed toward the stairs and said, "Your room up there?"

Middy took his hand and said, "Yes let me show you my quarters."

Middy gave Rick a brief tour of her quarters, but only nodded toward her bedroom door that was closed. She had left it that day without even making up the bed and didn't want Rick to see the mess.

She knew he must be wondering why he was there and decided to tell him. She led him back into her small dining area and they both sat at the table. She reached for his hand like she had always done with Patsy. She had learned this habit from her parents. "Rick, I know you are engaged and I know you have lived in Topeka all your life."

Rick frowned and said, "Yeah, Middy...What is this all about." He was beginning to wonder why all this delay in telling him why he was there.

Middy was smiling. "Rick, I've been with Patsy Holt for over six years now." She released his hand and looked down, then back to meet his eyes. "I'm lost being alone... and I need someone." She stopped and continued to look into his eyes.

"And you want me to replace Patsy?" Is that what you are asking me?"

"Well yes, something like that."

"Middy, I'm confused. Can you be more specific?"

"Yes, I'm sorry. It's not totally like Patsy. I want you to be my manager. I want you to travel with me and manage my concerts and appearances."

Rick was silent and then started smiling more and then asked the obvious question.

"You didn't know about me being engaged when you called, right?"

"You know I didn't, Rick."

"And if I wasn't engaged would this proposed arrangement be different?"

Middy blushed and said, "I guess we'll never know now, will we?"

This brought Jenny to his mind and he began to feel guilty with the thought of being with Middy sexually. "Middy," he said. "I need to call Jenny. She has no idea where I am." It was five-thirty, and he knew he would not be back in Topeka on time for their dinner date at seven-thirty.

"I'll just be in the library and give you privacy." Middy smiled at him as she walked away.

Rick watched her walk into the library and closed the door. He then pushed Jenny's number on his cell.

CHAPTER

Jenny had just gotten home from her shopping trip with her friends when she heard her cell and then saw Rick's name on the display. "Well, you caught me just in time, Rick."

Rick smiled and thought how he was going to tell her where he was, but first he said, "Just in time?"

Jenny laughed and said, "Yes, I just got home and was going to shower and be ready for you at seven-thirty. We are still on for dinner, right?"

He was so nervous he could hardly speak and said in a very soft voice, "Jenny, I need to tell you where I am and why."

"Really… What do you mean?"

He cleared his throat and wished he had a drink of water to moisten his dry mouth. "Honey, do you remember me telling you about meeting Middy Adams?"

Jenny frowned as she heard Middy's name. "Well, of course, we have discussed that meeting several times. It was actually two meetings as I remember."

"Yes, Jenny, it was two meetings…and today, I met her again."

"Rick Stone, this is taking way too long. Now, tell me what is going on."

Rick knew it was taking too long, but he couldn't just come out and say he was with Middy Adams in her home. "Jenny, you know how much I love you."

Jenny couldn't stand it as she raised her voice. "Rick, I'm hanging up if you don't tell me right now what's going on. What does this have to do with Middy Adams? Are you with her?"

"Jenny..." The phone was silent and he knew she had ended the call. He sat there and closed his eyes, wondering how he could convince Jenny that he had no intention of wanting Middy instead of her.

Middy had waited in the library for several minutes and felt like Rick would be finished with his call. She slowly opened her door and listened. There was no sound, so she walked into the kitchen and saw Rick sitting at the small table. He was still holding his cell phone and had his eyes closed. She wasn't sure if he had received bad news or what the problem could be. Rick jumped as she placed her hand on his shoulder. She flinched from his jump and said, "Oh, Rick, I'm sorry to startle you. Are you okay?"

His look was one of someone sick. His eyes were red and his smile was gone. "Middy, I've just talked with Jenny."

Middy smiled, hoping to improve his mood. "And she is okay?"

"Well, I'm not sure she's okay."

"Is she sick, anything wrong?"

"Oh, Middy...when I told her about you, she became upset and ended the call."

Middy wanted to show concern, but she actually found herself feeling a little relieved that Rick may be losing his fiancée. Instead, she sat down and reached for his hand.

"Rick, I'm sure she was shocked to learn where you are." He was now looking into her pretty blue eyes. She could feel his desire for her, at least thought he desired her.

"Let's have some dinner and we can talk about both of our futures. What do you think?"

Rick had no idea what he was thinking. He knew he was in serious trouble with Jenny. Then he thought how Jenny wouldn't give him a chance to explain. How could she not give him time to explain? He knew she loved him, but also knew she could be very jealous. He remembered the time he had told her about meeting Middy and how beautiful she was. He had also told her how nice she had been. Jenny's comment then was, did he think Middy was prettier and nicer than she was. He had told her that she was more important to him than anyone, including Middy Adams. She had listened then shocked him with her next question. "Do you have a desire to be with Middy Adams?" Now he sat there with Middy remembering how upset Jenny had been when he talked about Middy.

Middy's thoughts went back to their first meeting when Rick had asked her out and she had refused. Then over five years later, he showed a definite interest in her. Now, she had him in her home and maybe, just maybe, he would again have an interest in her.

They both started to speak at once. They laughed and Middy said, "Go ahead, I'm just excited to have you here. What were you going to say?"

Rick smiled. He was feeling better after having a few moments to think and put everything in prospective. "Middy, I am interested in discussing your proposal."

Middy winked and said, "You mean the proposal to be my manager, right?"

Rick flushed, his face became crimson red. His emotions were taking over and he was finding it difficult to talk with her. He was sitting so close to her and it appeared that she was interested in him. He felt like it wasn't just to be her manager. He finally said, "Well, sure. That is what you wanted to talk with me about, right?"

She just sat there, looking into his eyes. He waited for her to speak, but she didn't. Instead, she stood up and opened her arms. "Come here Rick Stone. I think you need a hug."

It was like their hug in his office a few months ago, but longer. They were cheek to cheek as she turned and kissed him on his chin. He turned his head down to meet her lips. They both closed their eyes and felt the moister from each other's wet lips.

Middy felt the security and love she had hoped she would feel. However, in her heart she knew she could never really feel the love she had lost from Patsy. She truly needed someone to be her friend, her special friend, but knew these feelings with Rick were not the answer. This gave her more questions about herself and what she really needed to continue with her career.

Rick, on the other hand, was beginning to believe this was meant to be, and all of his dreams about Middy Adams were coming true. At that moment, holding and kissing Middy made it easier to put Jenny out of his mind. His desire for Middy was beginning to overcome everything in his life. All he wanted at that moment was take Middy to her bedroom and make love to her. He thought she must feel the same but had no idea how Middy really felt.

CHAPTER

B ack in Nashville on the east side, Patsy and Agnes were having dinner in their condo. It wasn't as nice as Middy's house, but they both loved it and most of all, loved living together. They had started an animal rescue business and had built a shelter for abandoned dogs and cats, and Agnes had been able to have her dogs and cats now with her. The shelter was in Nashville, and Patsy always thought about Middy when they visited the shelter. It was just two blocks from Tootsies Lounge where Middy had made her singing debut. Most of the time, she was able to spend her days with Agnes and not think about Middy. She was truly adjusting to her new life and looking forward to spending the rest of her life with Agnes.

She still had Middy's cell number and scrolled past it when making calls to other people and places. She had just received a call earlier that afternoon from a pet food supplier they'd used in nearby Whitehouse, Tennessee. The name of the company was Middle Road Feed Store. She had allowed the call to go to voicemail and was now going to return the call. She accidently hit Middy's number, being next to the feed store number. She was shocked when she heard Middy's voice on her cell. She knew it was Middy and realized then what had happened. Middy sounded different, almost whispering as she answered the phone.

"Oh, Patsy, is that you?"

Patsy knew she had to answer her. "Yes…It's me…I'm sorry to bother you. I called you by mistake." Patsy started to end the call, but hesitated.

Middy's voice was stronger. "Oh Patsy, it's so good to hear your voice."

Patsy could hear the sound of someone in the background, a man's voice it seemed. Then the phone became quiet. "Middy, are you still there?" There was no answer and she knew the call had been lost. She immediately called back and got Middy's voicemail. She waited, knowing Middy would call her back, but she didn't. After an hour she still had not heard back from Middy and continued to get her voicemail. After leaving several messages she became frantic. This was not like Middy. They had talked since living apart. Even if Middy was upset with her, she would never fail to return her call. Patsy sat with her cell phone in hand and looked at Agnes.

Agnes had lost all interest in Middy Adams and wasn't concerned about her in any way. Patsy knew her feelings for Middy, but she would never stop loving Middy and worried about her more than she wanted to admit, even to herself.

Before Patsy could speak Agnes said, "You're worried about her, right?"

Patsy's look was enough to confirm her worry. She stood and looked around the kitchen before saying, "I'm going to check on her…come with me."

Agnes looked down refusing to make eye contact. "Be careful driving on the Interstate. I'll be here waiting for you."

Patsy wasn't happy with Agnes not going with her but understood. She kissed Agnes on the cheek and went out the door with car keys jingling in her hand.

The security guard recognized Patsy and smiled as he opened the gate to Middy's home. The drive was lit on each side, looking very much like an airport runway. As she parked in the circle drive, she noticed the house being dark. Middy always had some lights on inside. It was only eight-thirty and Patsy knew Middy was a night owl. It was usually mid-night before she went to bed. Patsy had kept a key at Middy's insistence and let herself in without ringing the doorbell. She entered the foyer as she had so many times in the past. It had been her home and she still felt a part of it. She flipped on the light switch, illuminating the room from the huge chandelier hanging from the twenty-five-foot ceiling. As she looked up toward the second floor there was no sign of any kind of light... total darkness. Her heart began to pound as she thought of what could be wrong here. What could be wrong with Middy? She slowly started up the stairs after switching the hallway light on, located on the landing above. She called out for Middy but heard no response. Middy's bedroom door was closed and as she knocked softly thought she heard a muffled sound. She turned the doorknob, turning it freely, relieved that it was unlocked. She spoke softly. "Middy, are you in here?"

The moan came from her bed and Patsy knew it had to be Middy. She rushed to the bedside and reached for the bedside lamp, turning it on. It was Middy, but not the Middy Adams she knew. She would not be recognized by anyone. Her eyes were swollen shut and a piece of silver duct tape had been placed on her mouth. Her hands and feet were tied with torn bed sheets from each corner of the bed. She was laying there, spread eagle, completely nude. Patsy screamed at the sight of her and could not imagine what could have happened. She slowly peeled the tape from her face and whispered softly to Middy. "Honey I don't know who could have done this to you, but you are safe now. I'm here and I will never leave you."

Middy was silent except for her low moaning and sobbing. She seemed unable to communicate with Patsy. Her eyes remained closed from the swelling and were dark purple from the trauma someone must have caused this sweet young lady. Patsy went to the bathroom and found a small pair of scissors. She cut the ripped sheets from her arms and legs and then pulled the remaining sheet over her nude body. She helped Middy sit up and held her in her arms. There were no words between them for a long moment. Patsy was thankful that she was still alive and she was there with her.

After what seemed like several minutes, Patsy broke the silence. "Can you tell me what happened, who did this to you honey?"

Middy only shook her head and continued to moan. Patsy knew she must be suffering from the trauma and sat quietly with her best friend, allowing her to have whatever time she needed to regain her composure.

Patsy had been with Middy for a few minutes and decided that she must get medical assistance for her. She had made no effort to speak and Patsy was afraid that she might have some kind of permanent damage. She thought of the beating she must have taken and the possibility of brain damage. She called 911 and asked for Emergency Medical Service.

Patsy had called the guard, advising him to allow the paramedics to enter when they arrived. They were in Middy's bedroom within fifteen minutes and were beginning to access her condition. Her vital signs were within normal limits, but they could not get any response from her. The decision was made to transport her to the hospital in Franklin. Patsy insisted on riding with the ambulance. When they arrived at the emergency room, Patsy Holt took charge. She knew everything about Middy's medical history and advised the staff that she was Middy Adams' manager. She also demanded that her presence not be leaked to the media. The hospital was used to country entertainers and understood the need for privacy.

An hour after being examined by the emergency room doctor, Middy was sent to a private room as far away from other patients as possible. Patsy was advised that a neurologist had been called and would hopefully come to the hospital that night to evaluate Middy.

Patsy walked outside Middy's room and called Agnes. She knew Agnes had no interest in Middy and could care less about her condition, but she needed to let Agnes know where she was and why. As expected, Agnes was unconcerned when Patsy told her about finding Middy and was now in the hospital with her. Patsy waited for some kind of comment from Agnes. After a long silence on the phone, Agnes said, "Will you be coming home now?" Agnes paused and made a small whimpering sound and then, "I need you, and I'm here all alone."

Patsy felt the bile coming up from her stomach. She

wanted to scream at Agnes, but instead said, "I won't be home tonight." She paused then said, "When you say your prayers tonight, I hope you will include Middy in them… she needs all of our prayers now." Patsy snapped her cell shut without saying goodbye and returned to Middy's room.

CHAPTER

Rick couldn't remember where he was. It was pitch dark and he could feel the hard floor beneath his body. His head ached and he could taste blood in his mouth. As he slowly began to regain his consciousness, he began to remember the last events before everything when black. He had been with Middy in her small dining area. They had kissed and he had wanted to make love to her. Yes, that was it. It wasn't a dream. Middy had received a phone call. They had actually gone into her bedroom, but what then? He kissed her again. A man's voice, he remembered a man's voice and he heard Middy say something and maybe she screamed. He couldn't remember any more. It was all gone after that. Now, he was in a dark place with a sore head and a fat lip. That was the cause of his tasting blood. His lip was swollen and still oozing blood. He slowly sat up and felt around, touching the wall. Tracing his fingers along the wall, he felt a door. He slowly stood and felt the softness of clothing pressing against his head and shoulders. It had to be a closet. He reached up and felt the clothes and hangers on the bar above. He found the door handle and turned it. It was unlocked, so he pushed it open and stood still unable to see because of the total darkness. He had no idea where he was and wasn't sure if he should make any noise for fear of being attacked again. Trying not to fall over anything in his path he decided to crawl along next to the wall and hopefully find his way out. Reaching another door, he stood again and felt for the light switch. Pushing it upward, the room was bright with light. It took him a few seconds before he could adjust to the brightness. He covered his eyes with his hands and slowly peeked between his fingers and finally removing his hands saw that he was in a large bedroom. He had only been in Middy's bedroom for a few seconds but felt this must be her bedroom. The bed was a total mess. Torn sheets were tied to each bed post and a roll of silver duct tape was laying on the nightstand. A blood-stained bra and panties were on the bed and looked to have been torn or cut. It was obvious that someone had been attacked in the room and maybe tortured before being removed or abducted. He thought it had to be Middy. She was one of the most famous people on the planet and some weirdo out there must have taken her. Rick wasn't sure what to do, but his first thought was to call for help. The 911 dispatcher was surprised to see the second call come from the same address she had sent the paramedics earlier that night.

Rick was standing in the large foyer when the police arrived. It was a two-man team and they both had a stern look as they walked in after ringing the doorbell. Rick was relieved to see them and started to explain what he knew had happened. The larger of the two men was an officer by the name of Bill Garrett, a sergeant and proud of his position on the force. His assistant was a younger man in his early twenties. He had no visual signs of his rank. Rick took him for a rookie. Sergeant Garrett listened for no more than thirty seconds before interrupting Rick.

"Sir, we have been briefed on what happened here and from what we have been told; a man was responsible for what happened to Miss Adams."

Rick frowned and nodded. "Yes, that's what must have happened…"

Garrett was talking again walking on Rick's words. "Well, Sir, you seem to be the only man here. The guard told us that a man of your description was with Miss Adams earlier this evening."

Rick was frowning now and his head was throbbing and his swollen lip felt very large. "That's true, Officer. I came here with Middy. She and I are old friends and I would never do anything to harm her, if that is what you are thinking."

"Well, Sir…what is your name?"

"I'm Rick Stone. Middy can confirm that I am her friend." Rick paused, looking from Garrett to his junior officer. "Is she okay? I'm so upset I haven't even asked about her…sorry."

Garrett was watching Rick and noticing all of his body language. He had made hundreds of arrests during his career and most times could tell when someone was lying or trying to hide information. He did have injuries, maybe from Miss Adams fighting for her life. He felt that Rick Stone was at least a suspect. The next comment from Garrett took Rick's breath.

"Mr. Stone, I am placing you under arrest and charging with the crime of rape and attempted murder."

Rick stood silent as he listened to Garrett quote the

Miranda Rights and felt the cold hand cuffs being snapped on his wrist behind his back.

The jail in Franklin was build years ago and was constructed of solid concrete. All the outside windows were covered with bars. The jailer was unhappy as he had been called in to open up for Garrett and his latest arrest. Sammy Sweat had been the jailer as long as Bill Garrett had been a policeman. They had never been friends and working together was a challenge for both of them. Sammy understood why he had to come in and open the jail. It was after two in the morning and there was no way to have the suspect brought before a judge at this hour. He would have to be locked up and make his appearance later in the morning. Sammy took his usual seat behind his cluttered desk and looked up at Garrett and asked, "Suspect's name?"

Garrett frowned as he always did when addressing Sammy Sweat.

"His name is Rick Stone and we are charging him with rape and attempted murder."

"All I need is his name for now; you can save your reasons for the judge."

Rick was standing next to Sergeant Garrett in total disbelief. He hadn't done anything to Middy and this gung-ho sergeant was accusing him of rape and trying to kill Middy. This was crazy and he had no way out at this time. He had asked about making a call on the way to the jail, but was told by Garrett that he could after making his appearance before the judge. He was taken away from his thoughts as Garrett took his arm and pulled him toward the hallway leading to the jail cells. Sammy followed them, pulling his keys from a large ring on his belt.

Rick was thankful to be placed in a cell alone. He had heard of all the stories about men being abused by hardened criminals. They had removed the hand cuffs. He sat on the bed and looked over in the corner at a toilet with no seat and no privacy. This was a night mare and one he'd never dreamed would happen to him. After hearing the door close at the end of the hall, he knew he would have to wait until Garrett came for him later that morning. He closed his eyes and thought about Middy. Her bed had shown so much violence, could she be dead? He wanted to sleep and try to ease the stress but knew that he would be awake until they came for him.

CHAPTER

Patsy had sat by Middy's bed since arriving there. She hadn't slept nor did she even think about it. The sun was beginning to brighten the haze that covered the parking lot just below the hospital room. Patsy stood, watching a new day and hoping and praying that this new day would bring good news about her best friend. An MRI had been scheduled for seven that morning and that would be more than an hour away. She turned to again look at Middy and noticed that she seemed more restless than she had just a few minutes earlier. Patsy went to her side and placed her hand on her forehead. "Middy, are you okay? Is anything hurting you?"

Middy opened her eyes and looked at Patsy, but it wasn't her eyes. They seemed blank; the blue color was grayer than her normal sparkling blue eyes. She almost looked like a dead person with no expression of any kind. Her breathing was steady, but no other sound came from her, however, her body flinched and jerked as she seemed to be trying to break the spell she was under. Patsy wanted to cry, but knew she needed to remain strong for Middy. Instead, she continued to keep her hand on Middy's forehead and softly talk to her. She wanted to say something that hopefully would bring her out of this coma or whatever it was called. She moved her hand to Middy's cheek and turned her head to face her directly. She then began to sing softly. "The items in an old shoebox opened up my heart." She paused and looked for some response to Middy's signature song. There was none. Her blank gaze remained fixed as Patsy searched for some sign, any sign of Middy snapping out of this awful state.

At exactly seven, as promised, a male nurse appeared at the door to take Middy for her MRI. He advised Patsy that it would take at least an hour and maybe longer, depending on what they found on the initial test. Patsy stood in the hallway and watched as Middy was pushed into an elevator at the far end of the hall. Patsy thought about Middy's mom and dad and knew they should be called. She had kept their phone number on her cell over the years. She made the call, dreading what she had to tell Tim and Mary Adams about their special angel, as they always called her.

CHAPTER

Patsy had hoped Tim Adams would answer the phone, but it was Mary's voice she heard and she had to tell Mary about Middy. She knew how much Mary had always worried about Middy and prayed that she could explain about her condition without upsetting Mary more than necessary.

Mary's voice was always pleasant and Patsy knew it was her when she answered the phone. After saying hello, Mary heard Patsy ask how she was. That was a normal question and one she was not surprised to hear. Patsy's next comment wasn't expected and caused Mary to quickly sit down on a kitchen chair.

Mary's voice was totally different, hearing Patsy say that Middy was in the hospital.

"What are you saying, Patsy? Is she all right? Where is she, what hospital?"

Patsy knew Mary would be frantic, but there was no other way to tell her. "We're in the hospital in Franklin, Tennessee, Mary."

"Oh, God, please tell me that she's okay."

Patsy hesitated, wanting to say something, anything to

calm Mary. "She's been injured and is now having an MRI on her head."

"Injured? Was she in a wreck? Oh, God."

Patsy sobbed, hoping Mary wouldn't hear her. "She was attacked, but she is stable, they just need to check to be sure there is no damage."

"You mean brain damage." Mary said as she almost choked trying to speak.

Patsy knew that was the answer, but said, "They are going to let me know within the hour."

"Patsy, you know we're coming. Please stay with her until we get there. Middy loves you so much and needs your support."

Patsy assured Mary that she would not leave Middy and ended the call. She put her cell back in her purse and went to the window and prayed. She was feeling so guilty for leaving Middy and moving in with Agnes. She knew none of this would have happened if she had stayed with Middy, where she belonged. She was sure Tim and Mary had no idea that she and Middy were not living together and wasn't looking forward to telling them about her new living arrangements. Patsy wanted to commit her total commitment to Middy but wasn't sure that she could tell Middy in her present state. She did, however, make a promise to God at that moment. She closed her eyes and prayed aloud, hoping that would make her prayer more convincing. "Lord, Middy and I have always trusted in you and have always been thankful for the life you have given us. I'm not sure how you feel about my sexual orientation but want to believe that you accept all who trust and believe in you. Whether you accept me or not for what I've done, I want to promise you that my life from this moment on will be for Middy Adams and I will never leave her again. I know there are others who live without a sexual partner and that is what I am going to do as long as I live." She paused as she heard footsteps approaching from behind her.

A small Indian doctor was standing in the doorway, wearing green scrubs. He smiled as Patsy turned to face him. He lowered his head as he said," I'm sorry, Ma'am. I didn't mean to interrupt your prayer."

Patsy was so emotional at the moment. She found it difficult to speak as she smiled at the young doctor. "That's okay; I'm just so worried about my friend. Do you have news about the MRI?"

The doctor extended his hand and said, "My name is Amad Singh and yes, I do have the results from the first test."

Patsy released his small hand and looked into his large brown eyes. "Please tell me, is she going to be okay?" His expression was serious as he clasped his hands together and said, "She has a brain injury and may require surgery. We need at least one more test to confirm that surgery will be an option."

"You mean there could be other options, like what?"

He hesitated, thinking before he spoke. "Well, it's best to talk about those after the entire tests are completed."

Patsy knew that more questions would not be answered at this point. She thanked Dr. Singh as he left with his promise to keep her updated with the results of the tests.

Tim and Mary arrived at the hospital at nine-thirty. They were directed to Middy's room and found Patsy sitting in a recliner in the corner of the room.

Patsy jumped up, running to Mary with her arms open wide. They embraced for a long time. Mary said, "Thank you honey. You'll never know how much I depend on you to keep our little angel safe."

Patsy's heart was breaking as she listened to Mary, knowing she must think that she had been with Middy when this happened. She was not only going to have to tell what had happened but would have to tell her that Middy had been alone with no one to protect her.

Tim came to Patsy and gave her a hug. "Yes, Patsy, we always feel comfort knowing you two are together."

Patsy asked them to take seats before she began to tell them what had happened. She stood at the foot of the hospital bed and began. Neither Tim nor Mary spoke until Patsy had finished telling them about finding Middy and calling 911 and ending up at the hospital. She hadn't explained where she had been when she came in to find Middy. She knew that would be an obvious question.

Mary was the one who asked. "So, where were you when all this happened?"

The moment of truth had come and Patsy had to give them the answer. Before she could speak, however, a different doctor appeared at the doorway. He was the neurologist Patsy had heard about the night before. His name was Charlie Grows and appeared to be in his late fifties. He introduced himself and shook hands with all three.

"I'm sure you are anxious to hear about our testing."

No one spoke as all three waited for him to share his information.

He remained serious as he said, "It's a blood clot in the

back of the brain. We first thought about surgery and wasn't sure if the mass was more than the clot." He paused to give them time to process what he had said. Then he continued. "Sometimes a blood clot can be dissolved with medication, but other times, surgery is required. At this point, we want to use medication and hopefully avoid surgery. Now, the good news is that she should be okay with time and rest. Her inability to speak is due to the pressure on her brain, caused by the clot. We see no damage to her brain; it's just the pressure from the clot."

Patsy spoke before Tim or Mary could open their mouths. "So, you're saying that she is going to recover."

Dr. Grows smiled. "Yes, I'm saying that there is no reason for her not to recover, but remember this, it could take time and we must be patient and let the meds work."

"And if the medication does not work…then surgery?" Mary asked.

Again, Dr. Grows smiled. "That's possible, but let's stay positive and keep surgery as a last resort." He looked into the faces of these three people knowing how afraid they must be at that moment. "I don't know you, but I am a fan of Middy's and I know how she feels about the power of the Lord. I'm sure she learned that from you. You can be sure that I will keep her in my thoughts and prayers."

Tim and Mary looked at each other, knowing how much their lives had been blessed and how much they depended on the Lord in everything they did. They knew Patsy felt the same. Tim took the doctor's hand and said, "Thank you, doctor. Please know that our prayers are with Middy and all the people in the hospital who are caring for her."

Dr. Grows then shook hands with Mary and Patsy before asking if there were other questions. There were none, so he left the room; leaving the three most important people in Middy Adam's life, looking at each other in complete silence.

CHAPTER

Rick had spent a sleepless night in the Franklin, Tennessee jail. A different police officer had taken him to the court house to appear before a local judge. Rick was so upset he couldn't remember the officer's name and really didn't care. He just wanted to get before this judge and tell him that he had done nothing wrong and hopefully be released.

Rick wasn't the only one waiting to be arraigned that morning. In fact, he had to wait two hours for his turn to appear. When he finally did appear, the judge asked if he had legal counsel. Rick told the judge that he had not been allowed to contact anyone as he was placed in jail directly from his arrest. The judge looked down at Rick. "You'll have to have legal counsel. If you have no one, the court will appoint a public defender to represent you."

Rick knew no one in Tennessee and was at the mercy of the court system. "I have no one your honor."

The judge requested that a public defender be located and told Rick to come back later in the day. Rick was again taken by his arm and lead toward the rear of the court room. He had no idea what to expect. The officer told him to wait in his seat and reminded him that the bailiffs would be watching him. Rick felt like a criminal for the first time in his life.

An hour after being in his seat, a young lady appeared and sat next to Rick. She introduced herself as Alice Ferguson, public defender and said she was appointed to represent him. He did feel a little better, but knew she had no reason to believe him. He sat and waited for her instructions.

Alice Ferguson asked all the obvious questions. Why he had been there, where he was from, his occupation and everything except his shoe size. He knew she had to know all she could about him if she was to help him.

After answering all of the questions she had asked Rick, he finally spoke. "So, is there a chance I can get out of here? I need to find out about Middy."

Alice had listened to him explain how he knew Middy Adams but had to also realize that celebrities many times had stalkers and for all she knew he could be one. It was her job to represent him and wanted to believe his story. She found it difficult to believe that Middy Adams had a man friend at all. She had read all the stories and rumors about Middy and her manager. But she had a job to do and she was going to do what she was getting paid to do.

It was three in the afternoon when Rick stood before the same judge again, this time with his court appointed attorney, Miss Alice Ferguson.

After telling the judge that Rick was pleading not guilty, she asked for bail.

The judge studied his notes and then looked down at Rick. "Mr. Stone, I'm going to grant bail for you, with one condition." He paused and looked at Alice. "Your client will have to remain in Franklin until this case can be presented to the grand jury."

The judge banged his gavel demonstrating his authority and said, "Bail in the amount of ten thousand dollars is granted. You may make arrangements with the court clerk." He looked again directly at Rick. "Mr. Stone, leaving Franklin, Tennessee would be a grave mistake. You are dismissed."

Rick smiled and said thanks as he turned and walked with Alice toward the court clerk's office.

Rick was surprised that his credit card was accepted to post bond. His credit limit was over thirty thousand dollars and he had more than enough credit line to cover this cost. Alice had gotten Rick's cell number and told him she would be calling him to advise when the grand jury would meet. She also repeated the judge's comment about not leaving town. Rick shook her hand and walked outside the courthouse, wondering where Middy was and hoping she was still alive and well.

CHAPTER

J enny could see that it was Rick calling on her phone
display. She was still mad at him but decided to take his
call. He wasn't very happy hearing her answer. "Well,
are you still with your Middy Adams?"

He cleared his throat and swallowed before saying, "Hi,
Jenny…please listen to me. I need your help honey."

She had no idea what Rick had been through and was
still unhappy with him. "My help? I can't imagine why you
would need my help Rick."

He knew he had betrayed her and she had good reason
to be upset with him. He chose his words carefully. "Jenny,
first of all, you know I love you." He stopped to control his
voice, again clearing his throat. "I am in a mess here."

"What kind of mess? What are you talking about? If
this is about your Middy, I'm not interested in anything
you have to say."

"Jenny, please listen. This does not involve Middy and
me. I have been accused of something I didn't do." He
paused. "I've been arrested."

Rick had to pull the phone away from his ear as she
screamed. "Arrested? Rick Stone, what in the hell are you
doing? You are driving me crazy with this kind of talk."

Rick took a deep breath and exhaled slowly. "Jenny, I need you and I do want to tell you all about my problem. Will you promise to listen and let me explain?"

Jenny sighed. "I'm listening."

It took Rick a long time to explain what had happened, including being with Middy when some stranger attacked him and Middy. He left out the part about kissing and going to the bedroom with Middy. Maybe he would confess this to her when he could see her in person. He needed her to be with him now and begged her to fly to Nashville and then on to Franklin.

Jenny was calmer as she said, "Rick I do love you and I know you could never harm anyone, including Middy Adams. I will be there as soon as I can make arrangements. Hopefully we can be together tonight."

Rick was in tears as he listened to her comment. He thanked her over and over and ended the call. His next move was to find Middy, but wasn't sure where to look. He was sure the police wouldn't tell him where she was. They believed him to be guilty of harming Middy.

He checked into a Best Western Hotel just two blocks from the jail. He told the clerk that he would be staying for several days, maybe a week. After checking in he went to his room and then took a long warm shower.

CHAPTER

Mary convinced Patsy to go home for a little rest, knowing she wanted to be by Middy's side when she finally woke up. Patsy was reluctant, but finally agreed. She had not discussed her where-bouts when Middy had been attacked and was relieved that the subject had not been questioned again. She was going home, but not the home Tim and Mary expected. Patsy knew they thought she and Middy were still living in the Franklin home together. As Patsy drove north on the Interstate, she was thinking how she was going to tell Agnes about her decision. She had no doubt about her decision and had made a commitment to God and herself to spend her life with Middy Adams. She knew their relationship was rare and special. Not many people ever find the kind of love Patsy and Middy had.

Agnes was having a late breakfast when Patsy walked in. She looked up from her toast and jelly and managed a slight smile. It was more like a smirk than a smile. Patsy did smile at her and went to her, reaching to touch her on the shoulder. Agnes flinched like she had been touched with a hot iron. Patsy stood back with a look of disbelief on her face.

"Well, Agnes, I'm glad to see you too."

Agnes was glaring at Patsy. "Oh, sure, that's why you spent the night with Middy instead of coming home where you belong."

Patsy pulled out a chair and sat across from Agnes. She placed her car keys on the table and set her purse on the floor next to her chair. "Agnes, that's what I want to talk with you about."

"What, your night with your wonderful Middy Adams?"

"No, I want to talk with you about where I belong."

Agnes knew what was coming. She knew Patsy and Middy had a special relationship but could never understand how anyone could love another person like they seemed to. She understood her love for Patsy and thought it had to be more than the platonic relationship Patsy had with Middy. Agnes waited before speaking; knowing what she said at this point could destroy her relationship with Patsy. She reached for Patsy's hand and received it without hesitation. She gave Patsy her best smile and said, "Patsy honey, you know how much I love you and I'm sure I know that you love me. Now, the thing that I really don't know or understand is the love you and Middy have." She paused and tried to cry but was unable to produce any tears.

"I need to give you time now with Middy. I know that you are upset and after being with her for so many years, you feel the need to be with her now, to comfort her."

Patsy pulled her hand free from Agnes' grip and frowned. "Agnes, you have no idea how I feel about Middy. She is the most important person in my life and will always be." Patsy did cry for real and with real tears. Her heart was breaking, knowing that her best friend was in a sub-conscience state. She knew she would always feel responsible for what had happened and all she could think about was what she could do to help Middy regain her health. There was no way she could continue her relationship with Agnes. It was over and she had to tell her so.

Before Patsy could speak Agnes broke the silence. "Patsy, we've had that discussion about how important Middy Adams has been to you, and you have told me that part of your life is over. You said it would be you and me, you're just upset now. You don't really mean what you are saying." Agnes moved around the table and put her arm around Patsy and leaned in to kiss her on the cheek.

Patsy pushed her back and stood up. "I can't make it any clearer, Agnes…it's over. I've made a mistake and I'm sorry. It's my fault that we are together. I thought I wanted to have a lover because I'm gay, but our relationship could never be what Middy and I have." She looked toward the door and then said, "I'm going back to the hospital and when I need to leave to rest for a while, it won't be here. I'll be back at home in Middy's and *my* house…that's where I belong."

Agnes did cry for real as she watched Patsy walk out of their condo and knew their life together was over. She wished Middy's injuries had been much worse, even death. Yes, she did wish that Middy Adams was dead and she would have been if the attacker had completed his job as he had agreed to.

CHAPTER

Middy was returned to her room just before noon. Tim and Mary were waiting and eager to see their daughter. She looked so different to them. Both of her eyes were closed and purple from the bruising. She seemed paler that usual and Mary thought she had lost weight since she had last seen her. The nurse advised that she needed to take her vital signs and then they could visit with her. All of her vitals were within the proper limits. The nurse smiled and left the room.

Mary went to Middy and placed her hand on her forehead. She then looked up and met Tim's teary eyes. "She's going to come out of this Tim, and when she does, I'm going to do everything possible to find out who did this." Mary turned her back and covered her face with both hands, sobbing.

Tim went to her and placed his hand on her back, allowing her to relieve the stress she had built up. He was just as upset as Mary, but knew he needed to remain strong for her. He hadn't seen her as upset since her brother had died many years ago. It had taken several sessions of therapy for Mary to return to normal. He hoped this would not cause her to return to that deep depression again. He wasn't sure he could ever understand the bond Mary had with Middy. After all, she had delivered Middy with her own hands and no one other than Mary could know what that feeling was like. Few people had an experience like Mary's and to know that her miracle child could be permanently brain damaged could be more than she would be able to handle. Tim wasn't going to let that happen. He knew with God's help and the skilled doctors in the area around Nashville, they would make her well again. He also knew from what the doctor had told them that time would be the word they would have to get used to hearing. "It will take time…please be patient."

Patsy was back at the hospital at two that afternoon. Tim and Mary were sitting in matching recliners as she walked in. Tim got up and walked to her, taking her in his arms.

"You didn't take much time to rest, Patsy. Mary and I are fine here; please don't feel that you have to be here all the time."

Patsy looked at Mary and could see the fear in her eyes. She had never seen her look so frightened during the years she had known her. She had heard some stories from Middy about Mary and knew that she could become very upset about people she loved. Her guilt returned as she thought how her absence had caused fear and heartache for so many people. She wanted to be there with Middy and her parents and only hoped that she would not have to tell them that she and Middy and not been together. She wanted that part of her life to be over and knew she would never be far from Middy's side for the rest of her life.

CHAPTER

Jenny did arrive in Franklin, Tennessee at 8:30 p.m. She was exhausted and mad when she finally knocked on Rick's motel room door. Her flight from Topeka to Nashville had not been pleasant. She had been assigned to a seat next to a man that weighed at least 350 pounds. She was pressed against the window and could hardly move as he took up his space and a third of hers. He also smelled like he hadn't bathed in a week. She pretended to sleep and avoided answering most of the questions he pestered her with during the flight. She took a shuttle from Nashville in a mini-van and had to listen to yet more talkative passengers. All she wanted now was a little peace and quiet as she waited for Rick to open the motel room door.

He looked awful. He hadn't shaved and his eyes were red. Her first thought was that he had been drinking, but soon found out that he was just upset and had obviously been crying.

Rick stood back from the open door and smiled at Jenny. "Oh, Jenny, I'm so glad to see you honey."

Jenny managed a thin smile and said, "How are you Rick? You don't look so good; have you been crying?"

Rick was embarrassed but answered her question

honestly. "Yes, Jenny. I've never been so frightened in my life. They have treated me like a common criminal." His lower lip quivered as he reached for her. Holding her tight, she felt the shaking of his body as he softly sobbed.

She felt sorry for Rick and knew he could never do anything to harm another person. She kissed him on the cheek, avoiding his swollen lip and ran her finger beneath his eyes, wiping away his tears. "it's okay, Rick. I'm here and we are going to get all of this straightened out." She looked into his eyes.

"You know how much I love you. All of this has been hard to accept and understand, but I have had some time to think since we talked on the phone. I know we are going to be okay."

Rick was so relieved to hear what she was saying to him. He was afraid he would cry again but controlled his emotions as he pulled her to himself again and held her for a long moment.

Jenny could see that Rick had traveled lightly to say the least. His clothes looked wrinkled and his usual smell of her favorite cologne was missing. From what he had told her, Middy fooled him into thinking that they were going to visit her mother's grave site. He had no way to know what she really intended to do when he boarded the private jet.

Rick wanted to buy some new clothes but decided to wait until morning when more stores would be open. The motel had a restaurant attached and after using Jenny's razor to shave, they headed there to have a late dinner. There was only one other couple dining when they entered. Before they ordered, the couple finished their meal, leaving Rick and Jenny alone in the restaurant. They both ordered coffee and a sandwich/salad combo. It was a little too late for a heavy meal. The coffee was warm and the caffeine gave both of them a renewed feeling of peace they needed at that moment.

There wasn't a lot more to discuss except for the upcoming grand jury appearance. Rick was dreading having to appear before a panel of jurors and fighting for his innocence. He knew a few lawyers back in Topeka, but none in Tennessee.

After finishing their meal, Jenny suggested that Rick contact one of the lawyers in Topeka and asked for his advice before going before the grand jury. Hopefully, they could recommend a local lawyer for Rick. They both agreed that this was his best course of action.

After paying the check, they walked arm and arm back to the motel room. They shared the large king size bed, both falling asleep in each other's arms.

CHAPTER

After a long discussion, Mary and Tim had agreed to check into a local hotel and allow Patsy to spend the night in Middy's room. The hospital provided a roll-a-way bed for Patsy. She slept very little and was up and down most of the night checking on Middy. There was no change. Middy did seem restless during the night but made no attempt to communicate. Patsy prayed continually during her vigil. She relived so many years she and Middy had spent together, remembering how they ended each night, telling the other one to sleep well. They didn't always say they loved each other, but both knew the love was there. Patsy wanted these times to return and would never accept the thought of Middy not getting well.

Patsy was surprised to see a doctor arrive at 6:00 a.m. He went directly to Middy's side and with a small flashlight looked into Middy's eyes. He had not noticed Patsy until she cleared her throat. He turned to her and said, "Oh, I'm sorry. I hope I haven't startled you, I'm Doctor Peter Connor from Vanderbilt Medical Center."

Patsy smiled and walked to the doctor. "It's nice to meet you, Doctor. I'm Patsy Holt, Middy's manger and best friend."

Dr. Connor smiled as he took her hand. "You won't believe me, but I met you at a concert three or four years ago in Nashville." He paused then said, "I was impressed then as I am now hearing how you introduce yourself."

Patsy frowned. "Impressed?"

"Yes, I knew that you were Middy Adams' manager from seeing you on TV with her and pictures made at Vanderbilt when you and Middy visited the Children's Hospital when Middy first started her career. So, when you made it clear that you weren't just her manager, but her best friend as well. I think that's very special."

Patsy was impressed. It pleased her to know that Middy's fans knew how close they were. "Thanks for saying that, Doctor. We are very close." She stopped and held her hand over her mouth. "I'm so worried about her. Are you a specialist of some kind?"

Connor nodded. "I'm a neurosurgeon."

"And are you thinking she may need surgery?"

He knew everyone worried when they heard the term "brain surgery" and wanted to put her mind at ease. "I'm not sure at this point, but if we decide surgery is necessary, it's not like major surgery."

Patsy was looking at him with a shocked expression. "How can brain surgery not be major?"

Connor placed his hand on her shoulder and smiled. "I'm sorry, I know everyone thinks anything involving the brain is major, and it can be, but not this type."

Patsy raised her eyebrows. "Not this type?"

Connor pointed to the back of his head with his index finger. "A small hole is drilled through the skull and then we drain the fluid to release the pressure on the brain. It only takes an hour or less and most times patients only stay for a few days in the hospital."

"And you think Middy needs this, not the medicine like they told us here?"

"Well, the medicine can work, but it takes a lot longer, and sometimes it doesn't work at all, and we end up releasing the pressure as I have described."

Patsy liked this doctor. He seemed so calm and very confident. She had no idea how this could work, but knew this doctor had to be one of the best. The Neurology Department was nationally known and she and Middy had known some people from Nashville that had surgeries there and all were successful. She knew Tim and Mary would have to be on board and was sure they would agree with her to have this doctor take over Middy's case.

Dr. Connor looked around the room then back at Patsy. "I will need someone to approve this, should we decide to go with this procedure. Are you Middy's Power of Attorney?"

Patsy was quick to answer. "No, Doctor, but her parents are. Middy asked them to accept this responsibility. My parents are also my POA." She paused, looking down then back to meet the doctor's eyes. "We always thought if we were in an accident, we would be together." She became silent as tears filled her eyes.

Connor gave her a few moments to regain her composure. "Then, I will ask you to talk with Middy's parents. They will need to come to the hospital and bring a copy of the Power of Attorney."

He again took Patsy's hand and said, "Your friend should do well with this procedure and if you and her parents agree, I would be honored to take care of her."

Patsy hugged Dr. Connor. "Thank you, I'll be talking with them later this morning."

Dr. Connor left and Patsy went to Middy bedside and placed her hand on her cheek. "I love you Middy and I want you know that this doctor is going to make you well."

CHAPTER

gnes Barnes looked at her cell phone and wanted to
call Jimmy Skaggs. If he had done his job as they had
discussed, Middy Adams wouldn't still be a thorn in
her side. Agnes and Jimmy became friends during Middy
and Patsy's absence. He had been hired by Agnes to help
around the house with odd jobs. Middy and Patsy had
agreed as they didn't want Agnes to feel like a maid. After
all, Middy had told her that she would be a part of the
family. She was Patsy's lover, but Agnes knew Middy had
never accepted the arrangement. Agnes never felt a part of
anything, except being Patsy's lover. Middy showed her
little attention and avoided her as much as possible. During
Middy's concerts Agnes and Jimmy had a lot of time to talk
and little by little, she confided in Jimmy about how she
detested Middy. Jimmy had listened and agreed with Agnes.
She was the one who hired him after all, and he wanted
to keep his job. He really had it made and did little work
around the house. He was more of a companion to Agnes.
They shopped together and watched a lot of TV. Jimmy was
younger, just twenty and single. He knew that Agnes and
Patsy were lovers, but at times wondered if he could interest

Agnes in having sex with him. Agnes was aware of his desire and thought of how she could use it to her benefit.

Jimmy Skaggs had moved with Patsy and Agnes to their new condo and helped them with the same kind of chores. Again, doing very little, but Agnes had insisted they keep him. Patsy had reluctantly agreed. Two weeks before Middy' attack, Patsy had gone to Austin, Texas to visit her parents and brother. She stayed for a week but talked with Agnes daily. By this time, her family was aware of her relationship with Agnes, but was not happy knowing their daughter was a lesbian. They never said that openly to Patsy, but she knew how they felt.

During Patsy's week stay with her parents, Agnes approached Jimmy with her plan to get Middy Adams out of her life, or more specifically, Patsy's life. She knew they continued to talk and was afraid Patsy would eventually go back to Middy.

Jimmy was listening as Agnes told him of the threat Middy was causing in her life. She had told Jimmy that she wanted her out of the picture. He wasn't sure what she meant by that.

She knew his desire for her was strong and many times noticed him looking at her and smiling. He had told her many times how pretty she was and what a nice figure she had. She knew she had the body to get Jimmy's attention.

Agnes chose the right moment for her seduction of Jimmy Skaggs. They had finished dinner and were planning to watch a movie on TV. They sat next to each other on the large sofa as Agnes turned to face Jimmy. "Jimmy, the movie won't start for another twenty minutes. I'm going to take a shower and will be back in a few minutes."

Jimmy sat on the sofa, thinking about making love to Agnes as he had most nights, but had no idea what was about to happen.

Agnes returned wearing a bathrobe and barefoot. Her perfume was wonderful and permeated the room as she sat next to Jimmy. She turned to Jimmy and leaned in, placing her hand on his cheek. "Jimmy, I never take the time to tell you how much I appreciate what you do for me." She paused then said, "I know how it is to be ignored and I don't want you to have that feeling." She had never had sex with a man and never wanted to, but this would be her opportunity to control Jimmy Skaggs.

Jimmy swallowed and managed a soft whisper, "Thanks you, Agnes." His eyes were glued to her exposed cleavage.

"Jimmy, I want to show you how much I appreciate what you do."

His voice was still just above a whisper, "Show me, what do you mean, Agnes?"

Without a word Agnes stood and turned to face Jimmy and opened her bathrobe, exposing her nude body.

Jimmy stood and took her in his arms. Agnes stood back, letting the robe fall to the floor. She then slowly started unbuttoning Jimmy's shirt and finally removing his pants and jockey shorts. The next twenty minutes were heavenly for Jimmy. Agnes tolerated her first sex with a man but knew she would now be able to use him to get Middy Adams out of her life.

Jimmy was exhausted when they finished. The excitement had left him feeling spent and completely satisfied.

The next morning, Agnes told Jimmy what she wanted him to do to Middy. He was shocked and had never thought about harming anyone. She had said that she wanted Middy to be out of Patsy's life.

She used her newfound power to convince him. She kissed him softly on the lips and said, "You do want more of what we had last night, right?"

He hesitated at first then said, "You mean we can do it, like when Patsy isn't here?"

Agnes smiled and kissed him again, letting her tongue brush his lips. "Sure, and who knows, we may take a long-time shopping and stop at a local motel."

Jimmy was under her spell. Her wish would be his command. "Tell me what you are thinking; what do you want me to do to Middy."

Now, Agnes was sitting and thinking about calling Jimmy. What had gone wrong? Would they trace the attack back to him? Would he tell them that she had asked him to attack Middy? She was worried; Jimmy was very naïve and insecure. He would be easily intimidated should he be questioned by the police. Agnes was afraid to call him, but wanted to know where he was. She had not heard from him since the attack. She also thought about how she had answered his question regarding what she wanted him to do to Middy. He was the only one who knew what she said and she would deny anything he said. Middy was still in the hospital and she hoped Middy would die there.

CHAPTER

Jimmy Skaggs was still in Middy's house in Franklin, Tennessee. During his time living there with the three women, he had discovered an attic space located behind a walk-in closet in Middy's living quarters. He was sure Middy had never found it as it was concealed by a large dresser placed in front of the small sliding door. Jimmy had found it one day while cleaning Middy's quarters. Middy and Patsy had been gone on tour and Agnes had gone shopping with one of her friends. Jimmy was surprised by the size of the attic room. It was floored and had a light hanging from the rafters. There was no window but did have a louvered vent at the gable end of the house. He had thought of telling Agnes about his find but decided to keep it his secret and had never told anyone. He had his cell phone but had not used it. He was so paranoid he thought about someone tracing his call and finding him. He had heard people moving about in the house the night of his attack on Middy and the next morning. Now, it seemed quiet, twenty-four hours after his brutal attack on Middy, and her friend. He had waited for Middy, thinking she would return later in the day after being picked up by a limo. He had no idea that she had gone to Kansas and would bring a friend with her. He had been given a key to the house while living there and no one had asked him to return it. That made it easy to gain entry, but he had to get onto the grounds first. He had a plan and it had worked. He had watched for Middy to leave, hiding in a small, wooded area across from her gate. The guard knew Jimmy and smiled as he saw him walk up to the gate. "Well, it's Jimmy Skaggs." He had liked Jimmy from their first meeting. He used to kid him about working in a house with three beautiful women.

Jimmy wasn't sure if his plan to gain entry to the property would work, but the worst thing that could happen was the guard would refuse to let him past the gate. They chatted for several minutes and the guard mentioned that Middy wasn't there a lot since she was living alone now. Jimmy did feel sorry for Middy but knew his new relationship with Agnes was more important than being concerned about Middy's happiness.

Jimmy had filled in for the guard on a few occasions when he had an appointment or other needs to be away for a few hours. This was his plan and hoped it would work this time.

He finally built up his nerve to asked, "Well, I'm just out doing some shopping for Patsy and Agnes. They asked me to stop by and say hello for them. They knew I had to come to Franklin."

The guard was flattered that they would ask about him and that Jimmy had come by to tell him. "Well, you tell them that I think about them often, and tell them thanks for asking about me."

Jimmy felt like the moment was right as he said, "You know I don't have much to do for the next couple of hours."

He hesitated then said, "So, if you have anything you need to do, I'll be happy to watch the gate for you."

Carl Farmer had been the guard for Middy and Patsy since they had moved in. He was very friendly and had always been agreeable to anything they had wanted. He did, however, have times he needed an hour or so to take care of something. Today, he wanted to get a haircut and stop by his bank. This offer couldn't have been at a better time. He had left the gate before when he knew they would not be coming or going, but now, he wasn't sure just when Middy would be returning. He smiled at Jimmy and said, "Well, there are a couple of things I can do, if you are sure."

Jimmy tried to not show his excitement as he smiled and said, "Oh, Carl, you know me, I'm always happy to help you out."

When Carl returned a little over two hours later, he frowned as he read a note from Jimmy. It read:

"Good to see you again, Carl. Sorry I had to leave before you got back. Jimmy." Carl wasn't happy that Jimmy had gone before he returned, but then thought, he had been gone longer than he told Jimmy. It was okay, the gate couldn't have been unattended very long. Carl smiled again as he thought of the nice things Jimmy had told him about the ladies.

Now, Jimmy Skaggs felt trapped in Middy' house. He pushed the sliding door to one side, exposing the back of the dresser. He waited for several seconds, listening for any sound in the house. He heard none and gently pushed the dresser out and turning sideways moved into the closet. After waiting again and hearing no sounds, he walked into Middy's bedroom where he had so brutally beaten her after hitting her friend in the head with a brass lamp. Middy had not been able to tell who he was, he was sure. It was dark and she had immediately turned toward her fallen friend. That's when he hit her with the same brass lamp. They had both laid on the floor completely unconscious. Jimmy had turned on another lamp near the bed and was able to see his victims clearly. The man was nicely dressed and very handsome. He dragged the man's body into the walk-in closet and then picked up Middy and placed her on her king-size bed. He was sure the man was out cold and took advantage of Middy Adams, Super Star. After removing her clothes, tearing her bra and panties in the process, he tied her hands and feet to the bed post, using bed sheets he found in a nearby chest-of-drawers. As her body lay there spread eagle, he took advantage of her, raping her in her own bed, as she lay there unconscious. When he had finished, he checked on the man. He was still out cold. He pushed him under a rack of Middy's dresses and covered him with blankets and pillows. He then sat thinking what to do next and decided to wait there, hiding in the hidden attic room.

It was two hours later when he heard voices and knew someone had come to check on Middy. He didn't know who and made no attempt to find out.

Now, he was alone in the house and wondering how he could escape from his self-imposed prison.

CHAPTER

Tim and Mary returned to the hospital that morning just after eight. Patsy had been anxiously waiting for them and stood up as they entered Middy's room.

Mary was first to speak. "Any change? Has she said anything to you, Patsy?"

Patsy knew Mary was always thinking the worst when it came to Middy's welfare. No one could be more concern or upset than Mary Adams.

Patsy hugged Mary and kissed her on the cheek. "She's still the same. She was a little restless during the night, but no change." She looked at Tim and then back at Mary. "A doctor from Vanderbilt was here this morning and asked me to tell you all what he thinks."

"A doctor, what kind of doctor?" Mary asked.

"Please sit down, you two. It sounds like good news to me."

Tim and Mary sat in the same recliners they had used the night before and looked up at Patsy.

She stood in front of them and told them what Doctor Peter Connor had told her. Mary and Tim were silent as they looked at Middy, both showing signs of concern on their sad faces.

Patsy knew how much this was upsetting them. She wanted to say the right thing and hopefully get their agreement to at least discuss the procedure with Doctor Connor.

Mary went to Middy's bedside and leaned over, kissing her on the forehead. "Surgery of any kind scares me," she said. "We do want her to get well, but really need to keep an open mind, however."

Tim was relieved to hear Mary beginning to accept the possibility of surgery. He knew he had to allow her time to process the idea in her own mind. They had been married over twenty-five years and knew when to give the other one that extra time.

Patsy turned as she heard a voice she had remembered when Middy was first admitted. It was Dr. Singh. He smiled as he approached her with his hand extended. "Patsy Holt… is that correct?"

His accent and skin color confirmed his Indian heritage. Patsy remembered how kind he had been on their first meeting. "Yes, Dr. Singh, it's good to see you again." She paused and looked toward Tim and Mary. "You haven't met Middy's parents."

Patsy made the proper introductions and then noticed a serious look forming in Dr. Singh's face.

"Well, I'm glad to meet you and also glad you can hear directly more information about your daughter."

Mary couldn't wait for him to continue as she said, "Please tell me its good news, Doctor."

He paused. "Well, it's not good news, but it isn't life threatening either."

No one spoke as they all three waited for the "news."

"Your daughter," he said then after more hesitation. "She has been raped; we found semen during the rape test."

Mary was glaring at him. "Rape test, why would you do a test like that?"

"We always check when there has been trauma. We were more concerned with her head injury and wanted to address that before telling you about the sexual assault."

Mary broke down and started crying. Patsy held her like she had always held Middy when she was upset. Tim stood, stoic, head bowed with his eyes closed. He was privately asking God to not let the worst possible thing happen. "Please, God, she doesn't need to be pregnant. She has enough to overcome."

Dr. Singh waited until everyone calmed down and then said, "The crime lab did take samples in hopes of finding a match."

"You mean with DNA?" Tim asked, as he appeared to control his emotions.

Dr. Singh nodded and extended his hand. "I'm sorry to have to tell you this." He paused. "We do have a lot to be thankful for however, your daughter should make a full recovery from her head injury."

Tim thanked the doctor and watched as he walked out the door. He then turned to face Mary and Patsy and cried, finally giving way to his emotions that had been tugging at his heart.

CHAPTER

ary, Tim nor Patsy had any idea that two detectives
were currently working the case involving Middy's
brutal attack. They were from the Nashville crime
unit and specialized in rape victim's cases. Clarence Upton
was the lead detective, assisted by his junior partner, Joy
Harmon. The department felt it was best to have a lady
partner on the rape case teams. Many times, the victim
would open up more to a woman than she would with a
man. It had worked for the department and Clarence and
Joy and had made a good team since their first assignment.

The first time anyone from the family was aware of the
detectives' involvement was when Patsy received a call from
Carl Farmer. He was calling her from the guard shed at
the Franklin home. Patsy saw his name on the display and
excused herself and walked into the hallway far enough to
keep Tim and Mary from overhearing.

Carl was friendly as usual as he spoke, "Miss Patsy, its
Carl Farmer."

Patsy smiled as he always identified himself, never
thinking about caller ID. She wasn't sure he even knew
what it was. "Yes, Carl, how are you?" She kept her voice
level, wondering why he would be calling her.

She heard him say something to someone but couldn't tell what he was saying. He then spoke to Patsy, "There are two detectives here, a Clarence and Joy…a lady detective."

Patsy knew the police would soon have to get involved, but with everything going on with Middy, hadn't thought about it until now. "They say what they want, Carl?"

Carl again said something to the detectives then said, "They need to talk with you, I guess."

Patsy listened as she heard a lady's voice. "This is Detective Joy Harmon. You are Miss Patsy Holt?"

Patsy only said, "Yes."

"Well, Miss Holt, we need access to the house, our crime lab has been there, but we still need to look around some." She hesitated for a moment, and then said, "We think it would be best if you could meet us here, are you available?"

Patsy knew she had to be the one to meet with them. She didn't want Tim or Mary to have to visit the house and see where Middy had been attacked. "Yes, I can come right away…I'll be there in twenty minutes."

Tim and Mary were in agreement for Patsy to meet with the detectives and thanked her for being there for them. Patsy was relieved as she thought Mary might insist on going.

When Patsy arrived at the front gate, Carl came out of his small shack and walked to her car. "Is she all right? Oh, I've been worried about her." Carl was holding back his tears.

Patsy patted Carl on the forearm. "She's going to be fine, Carl. I'll tell her that you asked about her."

Carl smiled and went back inside and opened the gate. Both detectives got out of their car and walked to Patsy's open window. After introductions, they followed her up the long driveway and parked in the circle drive.

The huge foyer seemed cold and strange to Patsy. She had lived there with Middy for over five years and had never really liked the foyer. They had not talked about it, but she didn't think Middy liked it either. It had been their refuse, a place of safety and security. Now, it was a place where Middy Adams had been brutally beaten and raped. Patsy felt a chill as she thought of that terrible night.

She was taken aback as she heard the male detective speak, "Where did the attack take place, Miss Holt?"

Patsy turned to face the detective and then looked toward the stairs. "In her bedroom, up there," she said as she pointed upward above the staircase.

Clarence Upton and Joy Harmon followed Patsy as she slowly led them up the stairs. She paused in the kitchen area, looking toward the bedroom door. She wasn't looking forward to seeing the crime scene again, but knew she had to give these detectives all the help she could. She fully wanted this terrible person caught and punished.

The bedroom looked the same as it did when Patsy was there two nights ago. Some items had been removed for the crime lab to analyze and hopefully gain some DNA. Both detectives walked around, looking with great interest and concern. Clarence then opened the door to the walk-in closet. Joy followed close behind. After flipping on the light switch, they noticed the dresser with a mirror at the end of the closet. Clarence pulled out each drawer, knowing the crime lab had already been there and checked it over, but it never hurt to have a new set of eyes. In this case, the new set of eyes did prove to be successful. The dresser was setting a little askew. Looking at the carpet in front of the dresser, it appeared to have been moved. Clarence pulled the dresser away from the wall and found the sliding door.

Jimmy Skaggs was horrified as he heard voices then saw the sliding door open. He was standing in the middle of the attic and had no place to hide.

"Well, who do we have here?" Clarence said as he pulled his revolver from his holster and pointed it at Jimmy. He could see that Jimmy was unarmed, but kept the weapon pointed at him.

Jimmy panicked, seeing the gun pointing at him. "Please don't shoot." He dropped to his knees and said, "I don't want to die!"

Clarence stood to one side, allowing room for Joy to enter the attic area. She quickly handcuffed Jimmy and helped him stand. Clarence backed out of the attic. Joy followed, holding Jimmy by the arm. Patsy was standing at the other end of the walk-in closet. When she saw Jimmy, she covered her mouth and gasped.

Clarence noticed Patsy's reaction and asked, "You know this guy?"

Patsy was too shocked to speak for a moment. Why would Jimmy be in the attic? Surely, he wouldn't harm Middy. She looked at Clarence finally and said, "Yes, he is Jimmy Skaggs."

"And how do you know him, Miss Holt?"

"He's our employee, was I mean." She paused then said, "He did work here, but has been with me and my friend, uh, in Nashville." Patsy couldn't believe what she was seeing. Her mind was racing, trying to make some connection to

Jimmy being there. She glared at him and said, "Jimmy, what in the world are you doing here, were you here when Middy was attacked?"

Jimmy remained silent and looked down at the floor.

Joy looked at Patsy and said, "We have ways to get information from people, we'll take him in and find out what he knows." She paused. "It's our job; we'll let you know what we find out."

Patsy wanted to know now and was beginning to feel bad about Jimmy being in the house. "I want some answers now." She walked to Jimmy and took his chin in her hand and pulled his head up, facing her. "Jimmy Skaggs, if you had anything to do with Middy being molested and raped, I'll…" She stood back from him and started crying.

Clarence placed his hand of Patsy's shoulder. "Miss Holt, Detective Harmon is right; we'll take him in and get the truth out of Mr. Skaggs." After a moment he said, "Do you want us to escort you to your car?"

Patsy shook her head. "No, I'll be going back to the hospital, but I have a few things I want to pick up for Middy." She looked at Jimmy again then back Clarence. "Please call me."

Clarence nodded and Patsy watched as the two detectives lead Jimmy down the stairs. She was sure he must that have been involved.

CHAPTER

M iddy was listening to what the doctors were saying but couldn't understand why they were talking about her. She could see their images as they stood in front of the bright light just above her. Then she felt a warm hand on her cheek. His voice was softer than the others she had been hearing. He said his name was Doctor Connor, she thought. Then she thought about Conway Tweedy, the country music singer. It wasn't him she knew. He was a doctor, he had said. She listened as he said, "We are going to put you to sleep, Middy and when you wake up, you're going to be much better."

Middy was saying to herself, "much better, much better." And then she was out. She wouldn't know any more until she would awaken later in the day.

Mary and Tim were sitting in the waiting room, drinking coffee from paper cups and keeping their faith. They were both upset knowing their daughter was in an operating room several floors above them having a hole drilled in her head. Dr. Connor had assured them that the procedure was routine and that Middy would be feeling better when she awoke. They had listened to him and had believed him.

Mary's cell vibrated and she saw Patsy's name on her

display screen. Before she could answer Patsy, said, "Where are you? Middy's room is empty and they won't tell me anything." She sounded hysterical.

Mary glanced at Tim before saying, "We're at Vanderbilt Hospital, Patsy." They had not called Patsy as things were moving so fast and they had just forgotten. Mary took a deep breath and continued. "Patsy, Honey, I'm sorry. We should have called you."

"Called me? Oh God, is she okay?"

Mary pulled the phone away from her ear as Patsy shouted. "Patsy, she's okay…she's having surgery right now. Please calm down and come to the main waiting room on the first floor of Vanderbilt…you know where that is?"

Patsy only sighed and closed her cell phone. Mary knew she was upset and wished she had called her like she should have. She knew Patsy would forgive her, however.

The surgery went as expected and Middy was moved to a recovery room. Dr. Connor called Mary on one of the waiting room phones. Mary listened as he told her that all had gone well and they would be able to see Middy in approximately two hours. Mary thanked the doctor and turned to Tim and hugged him. "She's fine and we can see her in a couple of hours."

They held hands and Tim said a prayer, thanking God for saving their special angel.

Mary and Tim were still in the waiting room when Patsy arrived. She saw them and walked quickly to them.

Before Mary could speak Patsy said, "Please, Mary, I don't want you to feel bad and please don't apologize…I'm the one who is ashamed. Please forgive me." They both cried as they embraced.

When they stood back looking into each other's tear-filled eyes, Mary said, "She's out of surgery and is going to be fine." Mary then took Patsy's hands in hers and continued. "Patsy, there are three people in this world that live in my heart. You are one of those and you know who the other two are."

Patsy couldn't speak. All she could think about was how she had deserted Middy, and now Mary was telling her how much she loved and trusted her. She had to tell her what had happened with Agnes and knew she would, after Middy was well.

Less than two hours later, a nurse approached them and advised that Middy had been moved to a room on the seventh floor. They took the elevator and went with the nurse to Middy's room. Her head was shaved on the side and back. A small bandage covered the surgery area. It was smaller than they thought it would be.

Middy's eyes were closed as they approached her bed. The nurse spoke softly. "Middy, your parents and Patsy are here, honey."

Middy opened her eyes and smiled. She was groggy, but it was easy to tell that she recognized them. Mary hesitated long enough for Patsy to speak to her. "Oh, Middy, we're so thankful that you are okay." She leaned over and kissed her on the forehead. She then turned to Mary and moved away. Mary smiled and touched Patsy's arm as she moved toward her daughter. Everyone in the room knew how important Middy and Patsy were to each other. It was a special moment.

Middy didn't speak but did nod and smile. The doctor had said that speech might not come quickly but assured them that she would regain her ability to speak.

CHAPTER

gnes Barnes was beginning to worry more about being a suspect in the attack of Middy Adams. She hadn't heard anything from Patsy since she left her and said it was over. Now, she sat alone in the condo she and Patsy had called home just a few days earlier. What if Jimmy Skaggs did say she was the one to suggest the attack? She could deny it, and would. She could tell everyone how Jimmy had wanted to have sex with Middy. She would tell the police or whoever asked her, that she had nothing to do with Jimmy's actions. He had acted alone, and if he did try to implicate her, she would just act surprised and shocked. The more she thought about the possibility, the better she felt, and he couldn't prove anything anyway. He was just a sex starved kid and let his emotions and desires overcome his better judgment. Agnes smiled as she finally convinced herself she had nothing to worry about.

The relief of not worrying about being accused of Middy's attack didn't change how she felt about Patsy. Agnes loved Patsy and thought Patsy loved her, but there was always the threat of Middy. She still hated Middy and really hoped she never recovered from her injuries. But she thought from Patsy's comments and actions that their relationship would be over no matter what happened to Middy. She knew Patsy felt responsible for what had happened to Middy and may not leave her again, if she did survive. Agnes wasn't going to give up on the idea of getting Patsy back. She would just be patient and wait. Time could always change things and she had plenty of time.

Agnes had her first chance to play the role she had been rehearsing as her cell chimed. It was Patsy. She was very calm as she told Agnes about Middy's surgery and how happy and thankful, she was. Agnes tried to show her concern and relief for Middy, but Patsy knew it was only an act.

"Agnes, I did call to let you know about Middy, but I have another reason for calling you." She paused. "Jimmy Skaggs was found in Middy's house."

Agnes was glad no one was there to see her face flush as she said, "Jimmy was in Middy's house, what are you saying, Patsy?"

Patsy knew how close Jimmy and Agnes had become and wondered if he had said anything to her about Middy. "I'm saying he was there...I saw him and talked with him."

Again, Agnes felt the heat on her face as she said, "What did he say?"

"He didn't say anything, but he has to be the one who assaulted and raped Middy."

Agnes had no idea about the rape and couldn't believe Jimmy would do that to her. "Middy was raped. Are you sure, Patsy?"

"Agnes, the doctor performed a test and yes, confirmed that she had been raped."

Agnes was silent as she heard Patsy sobbing. She finally

spoke. "Oh, Patsy, I'm so sorry. Do they think it was Jimmy for sure?"

"They have DNA from the semen and we will know for sure when they test it."

Agnes had to know where Jimmy was as she asked, "What about Jimmy, is he in jail?"

"Agnes, of course, he's in jail. Where do you think he would be? That's a stupid question."

Agnes wanted to end the conversation but had to show her concern for Patsy and Middy. "Well, I'm so sorry. Is there anything I can do, Patsy?"

"I can't think of anything now, but I'm sure the detectives will want to talk with you about Jimmy. You know him better than anyone else."

Agnes was beginning to feel panic again, knowing she had to keep up her act and convince the detectives of her innocents. She finally said, "I'll be available and you can tell them where to find me."

Patsy said goodbye and knew her next call would be to give the detectives Agnes Barnes' phone number and address. She knew how much Agnes disliked Middy, but could it be enough to make her want to harm her?

CHAPTER

Rick Stone's cell phone buzzed later that day. He looked at Jenny before answering. She smiled and nodded with her approval. He really didn't need her approval but felt better knowing she was supporting him in this dreadful time.

He didn't recognize the number on his display. It was his court assigned attorney, Alice Ferguson. He listened as she spoke. "Rick, this is Alice Ferguson…your court assigned attorney."

He just wanted to know when he had to appear before the grand jury. Her next comment took him aback.

"I have good news for you."

Rick was looking at Jenny as he asked, "You have good news?"

"Yes," she said, and then had a slight giggle. "Your charges have been dropped; you are free to go where you please."

Rick cried and closed his eyes. "Are you sure?"

"Yes."

"But how, what happened?"

"The police have arrested the person responsible for the attack on Miss Adams."

Rick couldn't believe what he was hearing. "That's wonderful...what about Middy? Can you tell me how she is?"

There was silence on the phone and then, "I'm sorry, Rick. I have told you all that I am permitted to tell you."

"Are you sure?"

"Yes." The call was terminated.

Rick was so relieved he couldn't speak. Instead, he took Jenny in his arms and held her and sobbed softly. All he wanted now was to keep his promise to Jenny and go on with their lives together. He did, however, need to find out about Middy.

Jenny looked into his eyes and said, "So, are we okay now? From what I heard; you are not a suspect now, right?"

"Yes, that's right and we are okay. I love you Jenny and want our lives to go on as we had planned, but..."

Jenny stood back a step and said, "But what, Rick?"

"It's Middy, Jenny. I need to find out if she is okay, they won't tell me anything. You know that I love you...I need you to trust me now."

Jenny walked to the door of the motel and looked back at him. "Rick, I came in this door yesterday and I can walk out of it now. I want to walk out of this door with you and continue with our plans." She placed her hand on the doorknob. "One more word about Middy Adams and I'm out of here. It's up to you Rick."

Rick couldn't believe how much she hated Middy and it was because he had told her about meeting her. She was extremely jealous and he knew it, but he had to find out about Middy and had no choice. He took a deep breath and said, "Jenny, all I want is to find out if she is okay and then it's you and me forever."

"You mean Middy Adams, right?"

"Yes, of course, Middy."

Without another word, Jenny went to the bathroom, packed her bags and then walked out the door.

Rick could only hope that she would understand and finally get over her insane jealousy. He was going to the local hospital and hopefully find out about Middy.

. He would deal with Jenny later.

CHAPTER

Rick found out that Middy was in the hospital at Vanderbilt. No one would tell him anything, but as usual, famous people could not keep secrets very long. Rick heard about her on the radio. It was just a dis jockey talking and stating that it wasn't official, but he got it from a reliable source that Middy Adams had brain surgery and was recovering at Vanderbilt Medical Center. Rick took a cab from Franklin to Vanderbilt Medical Center.

Rick knew her room number would not be made public, so he took a chance and went to the neurosurgery floor and walked the halls. He had seen Patsy Holt on TV and saw her coming out of an elevator at the end of the hall. He quickly walked toward her and spoke.

"You don't know me, but I am a friend of Middy's"

Patsy had had many occasions when people had tried to use her to get to Middy, so she was prepared. "I'm sorry; you must have mistaken me for someone else."

Rick stood his ground. "I know who you are and I must find out about Middy." He paused and looked down then back into her eyes. "I was with her when she was attacked."

Patsy gasped as she placed her hand over her mouth. "You were with Middy? How do you know Middy?"

Rick cried before he could continue. He then said as he sobbed, "I'm Rick Stone, she must have told you about knowing me."

Patsy put her hand on his shoulder. "Yes, Rick Stone. Middy has told me about you, but why were you with her? You live in Kansas, right?"

Rick had no idea how she could know where he was from. Then, Patsy explained how she had waited in the limo when Middy had visited him several months ago.

After Rick explained how Middy had picked him up in Topeka and brought him to Franklin, Patsy understood. It did make her feel worse knowing how desperate Middy was to have someone to comfort her. All of this had been her fault. He wouldn't be there; Middy wouldn't be in the hospital and Tim and Mary wouldn't so upset about their angel. She felt like crying, but knew she had to control her emotions. Middy Adams was going to be safe and protected as long as Patsy lived.

Rick stood back and smiled at Patsy. "So, is she okay?"

Patsy placed her hand on his cheek and said, "Yes, Rick. She is going to be fine. She hasn't been awake yet, but let me check on her. Maybe you can just see her for a moment, I'll be right back.

Rick watched as Patsy walked down the long hall and entered the last room on the right. He was so thankful and relieved to hear that Middy was okay.

Patsy was surprised to find Middy alone, and she seemed to be awake. Moving quietly toward her she could see that Middy was awake. She smiled at Patsy and extended her hand to her. Patsy took her hand as tears began to flow down her cheeks. "Oh, Middy, Honey I'm so happy to see you awake."

Middy pulled Patsy toward her and she leaned in to kiss her on the cheek. To her surprise, Middy kissed her also. Patsy was so overcome with love for Middy she couldn't express her feelings.

Then it happened, she spoke for the first time. Her voice was raspy and weak as she said, "I love…"

Patsy knew what she meant as she said, "And I love you too, Middy." Patsy ran her fingers through her hair just above her forehead. "We need to get your hair fixed, Honey."

Middy had no idea how she looked. The back and one side of her head was shaved and had a small bandage, covering the entry point. As Patsy continued to thread Middy's hair between her fingers she finally said, "There's someone here to see you."

Middy frowned and looked toward the door. Patsy wasn't sure if she should tell her about Rick but thought the worst thing that could happen would be for Middy to refuse to see him. She looked toward the door and said, "Rick Stone is here." She paused and looked back into Middy's eyes. "Would you like to see him?"

Middy's voice was stronger, louder as she frowned at Patsy. "Rick…No…Mean."

"Mean? Mean to you, Middy?"

Middy turned her head and closed her eyes. "Sad."

"You're sad?"

Middy started to cry and shook her head violently. Patsy knew she had made a mistake and felt terrible for upsetting Middy.

"It's okay Honey; Rick will not be coming, I'm sorry to have upset you."

Patsy looked up just as Rick was entering the room. She

quickly walked toward him, waving her hand from side to side. "No," she said. "She's not in any condition to see you. I've made a mistake Rick. I'm afraid you'll have to leave."

Rick stood still as he looked around Patsy, trying to get a quick glimpse of Middy. He knew she had to be upset but needed so badly to see her with his own eyes. He did feel better, knowing she was awake and aware enough to refuse to see him. He only hoped she didn't think he had done this awful thing to her. He slowly turned and walked back out into the hall.

Patsy soon joined him and gave him a hug. "Rick, I'm sorry you can't stay. I'm sure you do understand."

His smile and his demeanor told her that he did understand. He finally spoke, however. "I do understand, but please let her know that it wasn't me. I would never do anything to hurt her."

Patsy still didn't know all of the reason why he had been with Middy but did believe him. "Rick, I will talk with her and you can rest assured that I will tell her. So, please don't worry about that. You look so tired. I know this had been a difficult time for you also."

Rick thought, Yeah, you have no idea what I've been through, but didn't tell Patsy anything about his last day in jail and his very unhappy Jenny. Instead, he said, "You're right, I do need some rest, but please let me have your cell number before I leave."

Patsy frowned and said, "Let me have yours, I'll call you tomorrow I promise."

Rick gave his number to Patsy and watched as she added it to her cell phone. He walked out of the hospital and hailed a cab. He was going to a new hotel hopefully close to the hospital.

CHAPTER

P atsy stayed with Middy until she finally fell asleep. She had been fretful after the visit from Rick Stone. Patsy had been able to comfort her and reassured her that Rick would not be visiting her again. She would spend the night in her room but needed to take a break and have a snack. As she entered the McDonalds on the first floor, she heard Diane Sawyer saying, "Welcome to World News." She smiled as she thought how many times she and Middy had been in this same McDonalds when they were attending college at Vanderbilt. Her smile vanished as she heard Diane Sawyer announce her lead story. She stood and looked at the TV as Diane said, "Our lead story tonight involves one of America's sweethearts…Middy Adams. We have just learned that Middy was attacked and badly beaten. She is currently recovering from brain surgery in Vanderbilt Medical Center in Nashville, Tennessee."

Patsy had heard all she wanted to hear. She turned and walked out of the restaurant and took her cell from her purse. She called Mary Adams. Her main reason for calling Mary first was to let her know about the national news reporting about Middy. The hospital staff had promised to keep the information confidential, but someone must have leaked it to the press.

Mary was calm to Patsy's surprise. She listened to Patsy then said, "Well, I guess we shouldn't be surprised. It would have to come out sooner or later, so I guess we'll just have to be prepared to meet the press, as they say."

"Are you saying you will talk to the press, Mary?"

Mary laughed. "No, when I said we, I really meant you. You're her spokesperson, thank God."

They were both silent for a long moment. Then Mary said, "Patsy, Tim and I are going home for a day or two… in fact, I was going to call you a little later and tell you."

Patsy was shocked. "You all are going to Jackson?"

"Patsy, Tim and I know how much Middy depends on you and now, more than ever, she needs you and your special love."

Patsy sobbed and tried to muffle the sound, but Mary caught it. "I know you are upset, but you are the person Middy needs now. We'll be back in a couple of days, or sooner if you think we need to be there. Now, take care of our angel…I love you so much and am so proud of you."

The phone went dead as Patsy continued to hold her cell next to her ear. It broke her heart to know how she had abandoned Middy and now she had listened to Mary praise her for her loyalty to their angel, again. She only hoped that she could explain her desertion and most of all have Tim and Mary forgive her. She walked back to the elevator and rode to the seventh floor. She was to upset to eat and only wanted to be with Middy. She moved the roll-a-way bed next to Middy's bed and began her night's vigil. Middy's welfare was paramount in her mind.

CHAPTER

"Are you Agnes Barnes?"

Agnes had answered her front door after hearing the doorbell ring in rapid succession. Two plain clothes detectives stood looking at her, both with stern faces. Agnes knew this time would come and had prepared the best she could. She smiled and said, "Yes, I'm Agnes Barnes. May I help you with something?"

Billy Wilson and Glenda Staples were with the Nashville Police Department. The Franklin Police Department had requested them to investigate Miss Barnes. It was in their jurisdiction and they would not be influenced by the information known by Franklin officials.

Glenda answered Agnes' question. "Yes, we're with the Nashville Police Department, this is detective Wilson and I'm detective Staples." She paused just long enough to check Agnes' reaction. It was obvious that Agnes was nervous. "Miss Barnes, may we come in? We do have some questions and would appreciate you giving us a few minutes of your time."

Agnes stood back, holding the door with one hand. "Why yes, please come in."

Agnes wanted to act calm and professional as she motioned toward the sofa and chairs in the living room.

Both detectives stood in place and Staples said, "We prefer to stand, this will only take a few minutes."

Agnes was beginning to lose her ability to remain calm. She was thinking about her little friend, Jimmy Skaggs. He must have told them something about her and she had to be ready to deny anything he may have said. She wanted to say something, but her mouth was so dry she was afraid she could not speak at that moment.

This time it was Detective Wilson. "Miss Skaggs?"

Agnes found her voice even though it was raspy. "I'm not Miss Skaggs, my name is Barnes…you know that."

Wilson was hoping to upset her, using Jimmy Skaggs name. He knew it had gotten her attention and then delivered his big blow. "I'm sorry, Miss Barnes…You and Jimmy Skaggs aren't married, just lovers, right?"

It was too much for Agnes. She sat down on the sofa and looked up at the two detectives, her eyes filling with tears. "Why are you doing this? I haven't done anything to Middy Adams. Jimmy Skaggs is a liar and will say anything to cover up what he did."

Both detectives knew she had to be involved with Jimmy Skaggs. It had been much easier than they had expected. They had enough information to take her in, placing her under arrest for conspiracy with Jimmy Skaggs, to commit murder.

Agnes was soon in the back of an unmarked four door sedan, headed for the Nashville Detention Center. All hope of denying her involvement with Jimmy Skaggs had vanished in a matter of a few seconds. She had been happy working in a small animal clinic in Austin, Texas just a few months ago. Now, she would be facing trial and possible prison.

She had hated Middy Adams, but now, it was her lover, Patsy Holt. Agnes wondered if Patsy had ever loved her. She knew Patsy thought she was gay, but now she wasn't sure. The one thing she did know was that Patsy was the reason she was where she was now. The more she though as she rode with the detectives was how sure she was now, that Patsy Holt had used her and she couldn't hate anyone more than she hated Patsy at that moment.

CHAPTER

Patsy finally fell asleep on the roll-a-way bed. She had it placed next to Middy's hospital bed on the side away from the door. She wanted to give the nurses plenty of room to attend to Middy. Her sleep was filled with dreams, mostly about her guilt. She dreamed that Middy had never forgiven her and in fact, had asked her to get out of her life forever. Tim and Mary Adams had also turned against her and joined Middy in telling her to stay out of their lives as well. They never wanted to see or hear from her again.

Middy's fans and the news media accused Patsy of abandoning the person that trusted her with her life and because of her neglect; Middy had almost lost her life. In her dream, Patsy tried to explain what had happened, but no one would listen. She received death threats and was called a gay slut. She was considering taking her own life, knowing how much she was hated.

Just as she was thinking how to kill herself, in the dream, she was awakened by a sudden scream. Waking from her dream, she wasn't sure it was real, or where she was at that moment. The dream seemed real as she woke up. She couldn't understand where the scream was coming from. Then, she realized it was next to her…it was Middy. Patsy jumped from the roll-a-way, almost falling as she reached for Middy. A nurse came in just as Patsy was leaning over Middy.

The nurse was concerned as she saw Patsy's hand on Middy in the dimly lit room. "What's going on?" She immediately placed her hand on Patsy's arm and pulled her away. "What did you do to her?"

Patsy couldn't believe what she was hearing. She glared at the nurse and said, "Don't you touch me or accuse me of hurting Middy. I'm her best friend."

The nurse relaxed and moved back. "Please forgive me; I didn't know who you were, Patsy. I'm so concerned for her and thought someone had gotten in here."

Patsy turned her attention back to Middy. She had stopped screaming but was moving her head from side to side and softly crying. Patsy placed her hand on her forehead and stopped the movement. "It's okay, Middy, I'm here. You must have had a bad dream. Everything is okay. You're safe."

The nurse came back near the bed again and said, "Yes Middy, Patsy is right. Sometimes dreams can seem so real, but you're okay now."

As the nurse left the room Patsy thought, no one knows how real dreams can be, better than I do.

Middy was soon back sleeping soundly. Patsy moved a chair next to her and sat with her the rest of the night. She had no desire to go to sleep and risk that awful dream returning. She knew the only way she could be at peace with her actions concerning Middy's attack was to tell Tim and Mary the truth and beg for their forgiveness. She knew this wasn't the time, but she would tell them after Middy was better or completely well.

CHAPTER

gnes Barnes had watched Law and Order on TV for
years. In fact, it was her favorite TV show. She always
enjoyed the interrogation segment and loved watching
how the accused would always break down when being
pressured. Now, she was living the part and staring across
the table at two real detectives. She wanted to be strong and
careful not to admit anything more that would incriminate
her. She knew what she had said about Jimmy Skaggs had
brought her here and wished she had kept her mouth shut.
It was too late for that now.

Detective Billy Wilson smiled as he looked at his note
pad then turned his attention to Agnes. "Miss Barnes why
don't you tell us about your plan to kill Middy Adams?"

Agnes thought about a lawyer. She remembered how
the accused would ask for a lawyer on Law and Order. She
cleared her throat and said, "I guess I should ask for a lawyer."

"You guess?" It was the lady detective this time. She
smiled and looked at her partner, believing Agnes was guilty.

Detective Wilson said, "Do you have a lawyer, Miss
Agnes?"

The only lawyer she had met was Middy's lawyer. She
knew she couldn't use him. She remained silent.

"So, I take it," Wilson said, "You don't have a lawyer." He paused then said, "You will need one at your trial, but right now we can make it better for you if you'll just tell us the truth."

Agnes felt some relief as she said, "You mean reduced charges?"

"Something like that." Wilson said.

Agnes felt sure Jimmy Skaggs had implicated her, but she needed to convince these detectives that she had not been a part of the plan. "Let me tell you about Jimmy Skaggs."

"We're listening." Wilson said.

Agnes told them how Jimmy had been obsessed with Middy. Jimmy had told her how he wanted her, but she had rejected him each time he had approached her. He had become angry with Middy and had told Agnes he hoped she died. Agnes said she had told him to forget about Middy Adams. They had a new life with Patsy Holt in their new condo. She had no idea that he would try to harm Middy. If she had thought so, she would have reported him to the police.

Both detectives had sat and listened to her dialog, not believing a word. They knew she hoped this would place all the blame on Jimmy Skaggs and release her from all charges. They exchanged glances, and then Wilson said, "Miss Barnes, that's a great story, but we find it hard to believe. In fact, we are going to ask the district attorney to have a grand jury hear your case. As for now, you will remain in jail until then." He looked into her tear-filled eyes and then continued. "This might be the time to ask for a lawyer…you're going to need one."

Agnes Barnes was placed in a jail cell and would appear before a judge the next morning.

CHAPTER

The news media had begun to spread the news about Middy. It had been on all the networks, including CNN and other cable networks. Talk show hosts were interviewing everyone they could find in hopes of learning what had really happened to America's Sweetheart. Tim and Mary had been bombarded by the media. It was impossible to go outside their home without facing a horde of reporters, all with the same questions. "Can you tell us about Middy? Is she going to be all right? Was she raped?" The questions were endless.

It was too much for Tim and Mary. After a full day of this torment, they left home and checked into a hotel in downtown Nashville. Now they were only minutes from the Vanderbilt Hospital and knew they would not be harassed there.

Patsy had remained at Middy's bedside, sleeping very little on a roll-a-way bed in her room. Middy was still in the same condition. The hospital had her listed as stable on her chart. Patsy couldn't understand what that meant. She knew it was better than critical, so she thanked God for that. None of the doctors could explain why she hadn't regained her ability to communicate. She had only said a few words and they were all involving fear.

Tim and Mary started visiting Middy every morning, hoping their presence would have some positive affect on her. They talked to her about her early childhood, her desire to become a country singer, and then her quest to find her biological father.

The mention of her father caused Middy to react with a frown. She then started shaking her head from side to side and began to moan. The attending nurse heard her and came to her bedside. She looked at Tim and Mary and smiled.

"I'm sure you are trying to help your daughter, but whatever you have said is upsetting her. The doctors want her to stay as calm as possible."

Tim took Mary's hand and said, "Honey, the nurse is right. Maybe we should stay away for a day or so."

Mary cried as she looked down at her precious angel, and then said, "I know you're right Tim. Patsy will be here and she needs her now more than she needs us."

As they left Middy's room, they met Patsy coming down the hall from a well-deserved break. They explained how upset Middy had been and that they would not be back for a few days. They knew Patsy would call them if anything changed. Mary hugged Patsy and again told her how much she and Tim loved her and how much her love for Middy gave them comfort.

Patsy held Mary for a long moment, and then said, "Thank you both…Middy is my life and I will never leave her again."

As Mary and Tim entered the elevator, Mary looked at

Tim and said, "Did she say she would never leave Middy *again?*"

Tim had heard that too but made no comment. He had noticed how different Patsy had acted since Middy's attack. He knew she would be upset, but there was more. It was like she had a guilt feeling, but why would she feel guilty? And now hearing her say she would never leave Middy *again?* He didn't want to share his concern with Mary at this point. It may just be a feeling. He decided to keep it to himself and focus on Middy's recovery. He needed to direct his thoughts and prayers totally for Middy.

That night, Patsy was sitting next to Middy and watching her sleep. It seemed that she was asleep most of the time. The doctors had said that sleep and rest was the body's way of healing, and most important with a brain injury. As Patsy looked at her best friend and knew how much she loved her, she thought of Agnes Barnes. Agnes, her lover… Agnes, the reason all of this was happening. But she couldn't blame Agnes for this. Patsy had made the initial contact and wanted to have a relationship, a sexual relationship with a woman. So, again, she knew it was entirely her fault. She laid her head on Middy's bed and sobbed.

As she cried, she felt a soft hand on the back of her neck, moving slowly back and forth. Then she heard Middy's raspy voice. "It's okay, Patsy…please don't cry. I'm going to be fine."

Patsy couldn't believe Middy was talking. It had been four days since her attack and this was the first time, she had said a complete sentence. Patsy raised her head to meet Middy's weak eyes and saw her sweet smile as tears streamed down her pretty face. She knew Middy was back and so many prayers had been answered.

Patsy kissed Middy on the cheek as she had done so many times over the years. Middy put her arms around Patsy and held her for a long moment. She then whispered in her ear, "I love you Patsy. Please don't leave me."

Patsy wondered how much Middy remembered as she said, "I'm here and will always be with you Middy. I will never leave you…you are my life and I love you so much."

The moment was destroyed as Middy said, "What about Agnes?"

Patsy knew then that Middy had regained her memory. She only hoped that she could convince her of her true love and total commitment. "Middy, it's over. Agnes is out of my life forever."

"Forever?"

"Yes Middy, I need you to believe me…please."

Middy's smile was back again as she touched Patsy cheek and said, "I do believe you." Middy closed her eyes and was silent for a long time. She finally opened her eyes and said, "Now, I want you to tell me what happened to me."

Patsy wasn't sure if she should tell her at this point in her recovery. She smiled and laced her fingers with Middy's. "I think we should call your mom and dad. They need to know how well you are doing and will want to visit you as soon as they can get here. What do you think?"

Middy frowned. "I know you're right. They worry about me and love me. I do want to see them."

Patsy smiled and said, "I'll call them now. I'm so happy for you Middy."

Before Patsy could stand up, Middy held her arm and

said, "Then after that, you will tell me what happened, right?"

Patsy only smiled as Middy released her arm. She took her cell phone from her purse and called Tim and Mary. She thought the doctors must be consulted before telling Middy about her attack. She didn't want to say or do anything to keep Middy from recovering from this awful trauma.

CHAPTER

The next morning, Agnes Barnes was still in jail and had already heard from the grand jury's decision. She had been indicted. She had been charged as an accomplice to commit murder. Jimmy Skaggs had already been charged with rape and attempted murder. They could both spent many years in prison if found guilty. They would have separate trials with Jimmy going first. They had no idea what they had said about each other, but both knew the other one must have told the police everything. It would be two months before Jimmy's trial date and Agnes would follow within two weeks after that. Agnes knew she had no one to call. The only people she really knew were Patsy and Middy and calling them was totally out of the question. So, she sat in her cell and hoped that Middy Adams would die. She hated Patsy Holt for causing her to be where she was and felt that she could kill her if she had the opportunity.

Jimmy Skaggs had remained in shock since being arrested. He couldn't believe what had happened to him. He had been controlled by Agnes and would do anything she wanted, including killing Middy Adams. He sat and thought about having sex with Agnes and knew now that she had used him. He felt like he would go crazy if he had to spend his life in prison. He also had no one to call and like Agnes, sat and continued to have negative thoughts, including killing Agnes if he ever had the opportunity.

CHAPTER

Tim and Mary Adams sat on either side of their daughter's bed, holding a hand each. Middy started to cry and couldn't speak for several moments. She was so confused about what had happened to her but knew discussing this with her parents would be wrong. Instead, she thanked them for all they had meant to her. She reminded them of how they had been the ones to deliver her. She was so thankful to be their daughter. She then became silent and closed her eyes, sobbing softly.

Tim and Mary continued to hold her hands and prayed silently, thanking God for bringing Middy through this terrible injury and attack.

Patsy stood at the foot of Middy's bed and cried. Tim and Mary were sure Patsy's tears were tears of happiness. They had no idea how guilty Patsy felt. She knew she had to tell the truth someday, but not now.

Tim finally broke the silence. "Well, we have so much to be thankful for and I know each of us have thanked The Lord for this blessing and the many blessings he has given this family." He then turned to Patsy and reached for her hand. She took his hand and tried not to cry.

"As you know, we consider you a part of our family. We

can never thank you enough for your love and devotion to Middy."

Patsy pulled her hand away, turned and walked out of the room.

Tim and Mary exchanged glances as Mary said, "This has been difficult for Patsy, Tim. We have no idea what she has been through with this terrible experience."

Tim smiled at Mary and nodded. But he felt something a lot more than they could imagine had happened. He remembered Patsy saying that she would never leave Middy *again* and this bothered him considerably.

Patsy had never felt like she did at that moment. She knew she couldn't stay and listen to Tim and Mary praise her again for all she had done for Middy. She had to be alone and think. It wasn't just to think about the situation with Tim, Mary and Middy. Her time with Agnes had changed her life. She had loved Agnes Barnes. The only love she had ever known, the only kind of love she had wanted since she knew she was a lesbian. Now, her life was upside down. All of the plans she and Agnes had discussed during the time they had as a couple were gone forever. Agnes was in jail and would most likely go to prison. And all of this was because of Patsy. Poor Agnes never asked for a life with her. She was happy back in Texas with her job and her beloved pets. Patsy knew she had destroyed Agnes' life and in doing so, caused the attack on Middy.

As she had these thoughts, she walked out front of Vanderbilt Medical Center and stood watching people waiting for valets to bring their cars to them. She had left her car with valet parking but wasn't sure she wanted her car just then. She felt like walking and hopefully clear her mind of these negative thoughts.

CHAPTER

I t was eight that night when Patsy got back to Middy's room. She was surprised to find her sitting in the recliner in the corner of her room. Middy smiled as she saw the shock look on Patsy's face.

"It's okay, the nurse helped me to the chair and told me that I can start to walk some tomorrow if I feel strong enough."

Patsy went to her and kissed her on the cheek. "I'm so happy for you, honey. You've given all of us a real scare, but we know now that you are going to be fine, you'll soon be back to your old self."

Middy smiled and said, "Mom and Dad have gone to the hotel. I told them that you would be back tonight. They knew you would also, or they wouldn't have left me."

Patsy pulled up a chair and sat facing Middy and smiled as she looked at her head.

Middy placed her hand on the back of her partially shaved head and laughed. "What do you think, should I get it all shaved off?"

They both laughed until tears ran down their cheeks. Neither had felt this happy since Middy's attack.

Middy then became very serious and said, "You promised

to tell me what happened. Mom and Dad are gone now and it's just you and me." She closed her eyes and continued. "I have to know, Patsy. You have to tell me, please."

Patsy knew she had to tell her something and knew she must be honest with her. So, she began. "Middy, I know you don't remember what happened after you and Rick walked into your bedroom." She watched Middy for her reaction. There was none, only a look of interest on her face. "First of all, you need to know that it wasn't Rick Stone."

"How do you know that?"

"Well first of all, he told me, and the DNA."

DNA… She immediately thought of her DNA and finding her father so long ago. "Why did they take DNA?"

"Well, no one knows better than you how it works. It told them who had actually attacked and rape…" She covered her mouth, but it was too late.

Middy leaned forward and said, "Are you telling me that I was raped? Oh God." Middy's face had gone ashen, her eyes bulging.

Patsy couldn't look at her. She clasped her hands and looked toward the window. She had not intended to tell her about the rape, but she had. "I'm sorry, Middy. Me and my big mouth…I'm so sorry."

Middy continued to stare. "So, I was raped? Who raped me? Did the DNA show who raped me?"

Patsy had to answer. "Yes, and as I said, it wasn't Rick Stone."

"Yes, you said that. So, tell me… who?"

Patsy again looked at the window as she spoke. In a whisper she said, "Jimmy, Jimmy Skaggs."

Middy sat in complete silence, staring at Patsy. The

laughter they had shared just minutes ago was gone and now replaced with sadness, horror and fear. Middy thought about the possibility of being pregnant. Patsy had already had that thought from the moment the doctor had told her, and Tim and Mary. Now, she knew Middy had to be thinking the same thing.

Middy finally said it. "So, there's a possibility that I could be pregnant." It wasn't a question, but rather a statement waiting for Patsy's confirmation.

"Yes." It was all she could say.

"Patsy, I know you feel guilty about not being with me, and I know that you feel none of this would have happened if you'd stayed with me. Regardless of what you think, I want you to know that I could never blame you. I love you so much and know you love me. We don't know that I'm pregnant. I guess that is the worst thing that could come out of this…this; I'm not sure what to call it, tragedy maybe. But we'll still have each other and I know we'll be together after this is over. So, please believe me and quit blaming yourself, okay?"

Patsy leaned over and took Middy in her arms. They both felt the love and comfort they had always felt when they embraced. Patsy said, "Oh, Middy, I don't know how you can be so forgiving and loving. I do believe you and just hope you can continue to forgive me. I want us to spend our lives together, like we have always said. I love you and respect you so much."

An hour later Middy was asleep in her hospital bed with Patsy lying in the roll-a-way bed next to her. Sleep didn't come easy for Patsy. She wanted most of all for things to be back like they were before she left Middy. The guilt was beginning to eat at her so much that she wondered if she could ever be the same person. She continued to think about Tim and Mary and what they would think of her when she finally told them about leaving their angel, Middy. She finally sat up and looked over at Middy lying in the hospital bed and noticed the light coming in from the window. She had slept and it was morning. She knew she had to leave the room again. She had to get out again. She knew the nurses were there and would be checking on Middy every hour at least. She slowly stood up, stretched and slipped her feet into her loafers and quietly walked out into the hallway and almost bumped into a new nurse she had not seen before. They both said excuse me at the same time.

Then Patsy asked, "Are you new on this floor?"

She was very short and cute with blond hair. She smiled and said, "No, I've been off for a week and this is my first day back."

Patsy looked down at her watch and saw that it was time for the day shift, just a few minutes before seven. "So, you will be taking care of Middy Adams?"

The smile was still on her face as she said, "Oh, yes, and I am so excited to get to see her again."

Patsy frowned and said, "See her again? I'm Patsy Holt, Middy's manager. I don't think we've met you before, Miss…"

"Please call me Beth, Beth Hatcher. I'm an RN and have been here at Vanderbilt for just a little over six months."

Patsy was on guard as usual when someone she didn't know or had ever heard of, claimed to know Middy. It was her job to protect her, even if she was a nurse. "Well Beth, I know you may be a fan and want to…"

Beth held up her open palm and said, "Please wait, I'm not a groupie or whatever you call people who chase celebrities." She closed her eyes, and then opened them, and looked back into Patsy's eyes and said, "I met her before she was famous at my grandmother's house in Junction City, Kansas."

Patsy could not speak as they continued to lock eyes. It was Beth's eyes, those weird eyes. Oh, God. Could this girl be part of Middy's father... his daughter? Patsy had remembered Bill Hatcher's weird eyes, and Middy had told her about meeting with the Hatcher family while trying to locate her biological father...and had said the daughter had those same eyes. Her last name is Hatcher. Patsy felt this had to be her.

Beth finally stood back a step and said, "Is something wrong? You look like you've just seen a ghost, Patsy."

CHAPTER

Middy was as shocked as Patsy had been when she saw Beth Hatcher. Patsy had walked into the room with Beth and told her what Beth had said to her in the hallway. It had been so long ago since she had met Beth, but she did remember their brief meeting very well, a meeting that had allowed her to meet her real grandmother and two half-sisters. She had thought that she would never see anyone from this family again. But now her half-sister was standing at the foot of her bed smiling at her. Surely, she had no idea that they were actually sisters, half-sister. "I'm sure you remember being at my grandmother's house in Junction City, right?"

Middy smiled and said, "Oh, yes. I do remember, Beth. It's been a long time ago, but I do remember." Middy couldn't think of anything else to say as she waited to hear what Beth had to say.

"Well, as you can imagine, I've told everyone about meeting you before you became a super star, but never thought I would actually see you again. I am truly sorry for the attack you've had to experience and wish we could have met under better circumstances. However, you are in the best place with the best doctors here at Vanderbilt." She hesitated and then said, "I just wanted to let you know who I am and that I will be checking on you throughout my shift. I'm the charge nurse for this shift and want you to feel free to call me if you have any concerns or questions. It's so good to see you again and to know that you are going to make a full recovery."

She turned and then looked at Patsy and then back at Middy and said, "I remember you were looking for my dad for a friend...it was something about lost records, or something like that."

Middy remembered very well, she had used a ruse, claiming to be helping her friend from Vital Statistics, Rick Stone, to locate Bill Hatcher. She smiled at Beth and said, "That's right, and your grandmother gave me his phone number and address." Middy was then silent and thought to herself why am I saying all of this to her?

Beth's expression suddenly changed and her eyes filled with tears. She then said, "Yes, you do remember, I'm sorry to get emotional, but I lost my dad about six months ago and talking about him is upsetting." Beth did smile again and said, "Please call me if you need anything." She then left the room.

Middy and Patsy looked at each other for several moments before Middy finally said, "She has no idea about our relationship."

Patsy frowned and said, "And it needs to stay like that. The good news is you don't have to worry about seeing Bill Hatcher again. He's gone for sure."

Middy didn't answer, but instead started to cry.

Patsy frowned and said, "Why are you upset? You'll never have to worry about that weird guy again."

Middy glared at Patsy. "Patsy Holt, I can't believe you could say something like that. How would you feel if you lost your dad? What about me? What if I lose my dad? Beth is a very sweet person and has no idea what her dad did in the past. I feel sorry for her and I'm upset with you for being so cruel, Patsy."

Patsy was shocked. She had never heard Middy get that upset with anyone. Now, her best friend was crying and calling her cruel. She cleared her throat and said, "Middy, I can't believe you could think I'm cruel. You know me; I guess I just spoke too soon and without thinking."

"You got that right. Sometimes you talk before thinking...maybe you should count to ten before opening your mouth."

An hour later, they were both composed and slowly getting over the shock of meeting Beth Hatcher and Middy's outrage about Patsy's behavior.

They were both having private thoughts when there was a soft knock on the door and Dr. Connor entered with Beth. He was smiling as he walked to Middy's bedside. "Good Morning, Middy, feeling better today?" He turned to Beth and said, "I believe you've met Nurse Beth."

Middy smiled and said, "Yes, we met earlier this morning," as she nodded toward Beth.

"Well, I have good news. I am going to release you tomorrow morning. All of your labs have come back clear of any problems and I'm sure you will be happy to be home and away from all of this hospital confusion. We try our best to make our patients comfortable, but as they say, there's no place like home."

Middy loved Dr. Connor. He had been so kind to her

and she felt that he had saved her life. She began to tear up as she said, "You have meant so much to me, and I will always remember your kindness and compassion."

"Well, Middy, it's been my pleasure to help you and to get to meet you. You know, I am a fan." He smiled again and then said, "I did bring Beth in here for another reason and need your approval."

Middy looked at him said, "Approval?"

"Well, yes. You see, I want you to have around the clock care for the first week you are back home and I have asked Beth to be part of that care along with another nurse. She is well qualified and will be in charge of your care." He hesitated and looked at Beth. "So, will you be okay with this arrangement Middy?"

Middy immediately smiled and said, "Yes, I will be fine with Beth helping me and, I am sure she must be well qualified."

Patsy knew how Middy felt about Beth but couldn't help giving her opinion. "Well, Dr. Connor, I'm not sure we need a nurse at home, I can take care of Middy."

Before Connor could speak Middy frowned at Patsy and said, "Patsy, I think you forgot to count."

Connor and Beth had no idea what her comment meant, but Patsy knew and became silent.

Dr. Connor looked puzzled as he said, "Well, I think she needs close observation for the first week at home. Brain injuries can be unpredictable. I don't think she will have a problem, but if she did, having these nurses with her would make me feel better. And, it's only for a week."

He looked at Middy and said, "So, Middy, are you sure

you're okay with this arrangement? I want you to feel okay with this."

Middy smiled again and said, "Absolutely."

It was decided. Middy Adams and Patsy Holt would be going home the next day and have around the clock care, with Middy's half-sister in charge.

When they were alone once again, Patsy wanted their ill feelings to go away. "Middy, I know this is your decision and I have been wrong to try to take control. Please forgive me."

Middy was still unhappy and sad with everything that had happened to her in the past several days. She knew Patsy wanted to protect her, but she did have feelings for Beth and couldn't understand Patsy acting so cruel.

Patsy sat next to Middy and said, "You know, we've never had a cross word since we met. It seems that everything I do or say just causes more problems for us."

"Well, Patsy, feeling sorry for yourself isn't going to help either. Let's put all of this behind us and get back to some kind of normal life."

Patsy placed her hand on Middy's cheek and said, "I agree, and I won't say any more about Beth or this arrangement for your care at home."

CHAPTER

Agnes Barnes finally had a lawyer and because of the offence being against Middy Adams, she was getting her services pro bono. She had a court appointed attorney and would not have to worry about the expense of a lawyer.

Sally Stevens was just out of law school and needed the exposure to the public to hopefully make a name for her. She knew if this case went to trial, she would be in the news and on TV. This would be her first case to handle on her own and she was very excited to have this opportunity. She had worked as a paralegal during law school and had worked behind the scenes in several trials, but none as important as this one.

Now, Sally was sitting with Agnes in a holding room at the county jail, hoping to plan a defense to clear her client. As she looked at Agnes, she wondered if Agnes had really asked Jimmy Skaggs to kill Middy Adams. She had learned in law school and working as a paralegal to believe her client, even if she had doubts about their actions.

Agnes looked tired and unkempt. Her hair was uncombed and looked dirty from the time she had spent in the county jail.

Sally wanted to put Agnes at ease with her presents and hoped to question her without upsetting her.

She smiled and said, "My name is Sally Stevens and I have agreed to handle your case pro bono. Do you know what that means?"

Agnes looked at her and frowned. "I am in jail, but I'm not stupid, yes I do know what it means…a free service to me, right?"

Sally realized that she had started the conversation all wrong and said, "I'm sorry Agnes. I didn't mean to talk down to you." She paused and looked down at her note pad and then back at Agnes. "This will be my first case to handle alone, and I may be about as nervous as you are, Agnes. Please forgive me and let me start over."

Agnes continued to frown but make no comment.

Sally studied her notes for a few moments and then said, "You are charged with a felony and could receive a long sentence in prison. Now, it's going to be my job to convince a jury that you're not guilty of these charges."

"And just how do you propose to do that, Sally?"

Sally didn't know at that point but wasn't about to admit that to Agnes. "When I gather all of the information, including your account of what happened, I'm sure we will have a very strong defense."

Agnes was not feeling good about this young, inexperienced lawyer, but without money to pay for a seasoned lawyer, she had no choice at this point. She kept her focus on Sally but made no comment.

Sally shifted in her chair and started her questions. "Please tell me how you and Patsy met."

Agnes knew this was going to be a long process, but knew

she had to let her lawyer know all about her relationship with Patsy. Agnes left nothing out and told Sally how she had met Patsy, and had known each other in high school, and finally why they were together. As she said to Sally in her last statement, "We were lovers. And that's how I met Middy Adams.

It had been rumored about the relationship between Agnes and Middy's manager, Patsy Holt. This was the first confirmation of their relationship. Sally and Agnes both seemed to be more relaxed with each other after Agnes had shared her involvement with Patsy and Middy.

Sally wanted to be as gentle as she could be, but knew she had to ask some of the difficult questions as she said, "So, do you think Middy Adams was unhappy with your relationship with her manager...Patsy Holt?"

"Unhappy is hardly the word I would use. She was very angry and never accepted me or the relationship Patsy and I had."

"Did Middy tell you she was unhappy with this arrangement?"

"She didn't have to tell me. She did tell Patsy and it was obvious to me."

"So, at some point in your relationship with Patsy the two of you moved out of Middy's house in Franklin. Is that right?"

"Yes, Patsy and I did move out, but the house belonged to both of them. They have the deed in both names."

"Oh, and Patsy didn't mind giving up her interest?"

"We were lovers and our love for each other meant more to us than any material thing. "I don't know for sure that she has given up her interest. I'm sure you don't understand that kind of relationship, Sally."

Sally waited for a moment, looking down at her note pad, and then said, "I may know more than you would think." She looked up at Agnes and said, "I want to talk about Jimmy Skaggs."

Agnes looked away and closed her eyes. She knew this was going to be the most difficult part to discuss. She had no idea what Jimmy had told the district attorney but felt sure that he had implicated her. She slowly turned back to face Sally and opened her eyes and said, "I knew this was coming, so ask away."

Sally didn't hesitate. "Did you ask Jimmy Skaggs to harm Middy Adams in any way?"

Agnes looked directly into Sally's eyes as she said, "I did not."

"So, you had nothing to do with Jimmy's actions?"

"Nothing at all."

"Agnes, you know the charges against you are that you asked Jimmy to harm Middy, right?"

"Like I told you a few minutes ago, I'm not stupid, yes I know what the charges are. But I'm not guilty, okay." Agnes covered her face with both hands and sobbed.

Sally thought it best to end the interview at this point and maybe continue the next day. She waited for Agnes to regain her composure and said, "Agnes, we've made a lot of progress today. I think we should stop for today and continue tomorrow. Are you okay with that?"

Agnes nodded and said, "Yes, thank you, Sally."

Sally felt attracted to Agnes and wanted to hug her but thought it best to shake her hand instead. After releasing her hand, she left the holding room, hoping their next session would bring better evidence to help her first client.

CHAPTER

After a week in the Vanderbilt Medical Center Hospital, Middy was finally home with Patsy. They had agreed for Middy to stay on the first floor for two reasons: First the convenience of not having to go up and down the stairs and most of all, to keep Middy out of her bedroom where she had been so brutally attacked and almost killed. Beth Hatcher would occupy the second floor and use Middy's bedroom. Middy and Patsy had asked her to move in with them for the week she had planned to stay. Dr. Connor had agreed to limit the nurse staff to Beth only since she would be staying at the house for the week.

Patsy had the entire house cleaned during their stay at the hospital. She had also had Middy's bedroom furniture removed and replaced with a new bed and all new furniture. She wasn't sure if Middy would want to go back there, but wanted it changed if she decided to. It had a totally different look.

Patsy had a bedroom downstairs and she wanted Middy to have it as it was nicer than their guest bedroom. Middy had agreed, knowing this was what Patsy wanted. Patsy also insisted that she stay in the same room with Middy for the first night. Again, Middy agreed with her best friend's wishes.

After the first night, the first day back home felt strange to both Middy and Patsy. Beth was in the kitchen when they both walked in. They were surprised to see that Beth had made coffee and was sitting at the dining room table having a cup. She stood up and smiled at both of them. "Well, good morning, ladies. I hope you slept well. I did take the liberty of checking in on you during the night and you both seemed to be sleeping soundly."

Middy and Patsy exchanged glances and Patsy said, "Well, I guess we're both exhausted from the stay in the hospital. Thanks for checking on us, Beth."

"Well, that's why I'm here." She smiled and said, "You know, doctor's orders."

Patsy walked to the coffee pot on the counter and filled two cups as Middy sat down and looked up at Beth. "Thanks for making the coffee. You don't have to be a maid also, Beth."

"Oh, I know, I just want to help anyway I can during your recovery, Middy." She then sat down across from Middy.

Patsy set a cup of coffee in front of Middy and stood looking at both of the ladies, knowing that she and Middy knew who Beth was to Middy, but felt sure that Beth had no idea. She wanted Beth to be out of their lives, but knew they had her for a week and must make the best of it.

Patsy had called their housekeeper from Vanderbilt and had asked her to stock the kitchen with fresh groceries. The housekeeper had done a good job and the kitchen was fully stocked with the food items Middy and Patsy were used to.

No one was very hungry that morning and all three had yogurt and a cup of fresh fruit. Later, Beth checked Middy's vital signs and everything was in the normal limits. It was a good start for their first day together.

Later in the morning, Patsy went to take a shower and Middy wanted to try to do something with her hair. The shaved spot on the back of her head made it impossible to cover up. Beth saw her looking in the mirror and asked if she could take a look at her hair. Middy was pleased that she wanted to help her. Beth suggested that they cut it very short all over and when it did start to grow out it wouldn't take as long to fill in. Middy was surprised that Beth could cut her hair and make it look so much better.

"Well, Beth, if you had not decided to become a nurse, you could have been a hairdresser."

Beth laughed and said, "That's funny that you would say that I wanted to be a hair dresser when I was younger, but my dad…" She stopped and then said, "Oh, you don't want to hear about me. I'm sorry, Middy."

Middy turned and looked at Beth. "Yes, I do want to hear about you. I believe in people's dreams and know they can come true. It did for me. Your dad wanted you to be a nurse?"

Beth's eyes started to fill with tears as she said, "Well, yes he did, and I did it mostly because he encouraged me to be a nurse. He always told me and my siblings to help people anyway we could. He had a passion for helping people and told me that being a nurse would give me that ability." Beth took a tissue from the dressing table and dabbed at her eyes and then said, "I wanted him to follow my career and to know that he had been the reason I am a nurse, but now he can't." She sobbed again and said, "He died just before I started here, at Vanderbilt."

Middy took Beth's hand and said, "Beth, I'm sorry. I'm sorry you lost your father and I'm sorry I caused you to have to relive your loss. Please forgive me, Beth."

Beth looked at Middy and said, "It's okay. There's nothing to forgive. Please excuse me." She turned and walk out of the room.

Middy sat and stared at her reflection in the dressing table mirror, remembering the ugly face of her and Beth's father as she sat across from him in his office in Bakersfield, California. It had been over a year since she had made her visit to actually meet her real father. She had told him she never wanted to see him again, and had meant it. Now, one of his daughters and her half-sister was spending a week with her in her home. She couldn't help but feel sad for Beth. It was her dad and she would never believe what he had done in that old farmhouse so many years ago.

Beth was back after several minutes and looking fresh and smiling. "Okay, Miss Middy Adams, what do you think of your new hair style?"

Middy knew she wanted to change the subject and ran her fingers through her short hair and said, "Well, it's different, but I do like it. Thanks for shaping it up."

They both laughed and then Middy stood and put her arms around Beth and said, "I'm glad you're here and glad to see you again after all these years. I'm also glad you decided to become a nurse and know you will do great things."

"Thank you, Middy. You are just as nice as you were when we first met in my grandmother's house back in Junction City, Kansas. Becoming the great star that you are hasn't changed you. I will always cherish these few days I'll be able to share with you. You have already done many great things for so many people and I know you will continue to be a great influence on everyone you encounter.

They hugged again and Beth said, "I'll be upstairs if you need me."

Middy smiled as she watched Beth leave the room again, knowing she was feeling better emotionally.

Middy was still looking at the open doorway when Patsy returned from her shower. Patsy walked into the room and looked at the open door also and said, "What's happening? Where's Beth?"

"She just went upstairs to rest, I guess. What do you think about my haircut?"

"You let Beth cut your hair?"

Middy looked surprised as she said, "You have a problem with her cutting my hair?"

Patsy could tell that Middy was beginning to have different feelings for Beth and really didn't like it. She wanted Beth gone and was concerned that Middy was about to tell Beth the truth about their relationship. Patsy went to the kitchen and got another cup of coffee.

CHAPTER

T he next morning, Sally Stevens had an appointment
with the District Attorney in Nashville. She had met
him once and he seemed nice enough then, but she
knew when it came to the law, he could be a tough guy.

Her appointment was at nine that morning and she was
thirty minutes early. The DA's receptionist had welcomed
Sally and asked for her cell phone number. She explained
that the DA wanted all phone numbers from lawyers he had
met with. Sally gave her the number and watched as she
entered it into the computer. She then offered Sally a cup
of coffee which she declined. Instead, she flipped through
the pages of an old Readers Digest Magazines and tried to
calm her nerves.

At nine fifteen, the receptionist's phone buzzed. She
answered and said, "Yes Sir. She's waiting to see you, Mr.
Tabor." She then replaced the phone and said, "Mr. Tabor
will see you now, Miss Stevens. Sally thanked her and
walked to the door and knocked softly. She then heard the
deep voice of Tabor asking her to come in.

Charles Tabor had been District Attorney for just over
ten years and was known as being fair, but demanded facts,
good facts before he would agree to anything other than

the original charges. Sally knew all about his record from hearing stories from other lawyers and friends she had been with in law school. She hoped she was ready for this challenge. She extended her hand as he stood up and took hers.

He smiled and said, "I'm glad to meet you, Miss Stevens. Please have a seat."

Sally sat and said, "Thank you Sir for seeing me." She paused and gave him her best smile and said, "It is an honor to meet you, Mr. Tabor."

He smiled, knowing she was nervous. "You represent Agnes Barnes, is that correct?"

"Yes, Sir, I'm sure you know about her charges."

"It's my job to know about all charges brought in the county, Miss Stevens."

Sally blushed, looked down at her hands and then back to meet his stern look.

He knew he had embarrassed her and gave her a moment to recover, and then said, "So, has your client confessed to the charges?"

Sally could feel her cheek tremble as she said, "No, I mean she is innocent, Sir."

"So, why are we here? If she is going to plead not guilty, trial is the next move. Surely you know that Miss Stevens."

Sally felt like she might be sick. This was a lot more intimidating than she thought it would be. She knew she had to control her feelings and be professional. She was a lawyer and needed to act like one. She cleared her throat and said, "Sir, this is my first case and I've started this discussion all wrong. Please allow me to explain why I am here."

He looked at her for a long moment and then said, "I

know you are nervous, and I also know handling your first case is very challenging." He smiled and then said, "I've been there and I will never forget my first case. So, now, relax. I'm listening."

Sally felt like she had just been given a new lease on life. She smiled and said, "Thank you. I want to discuss a plea agreement for my client. I know I said she is innocent and I believe her, but after hearing her version of what happened and what I've learned from her charges, well…"

"You think she would lose in a trial. Is that what you are thinking?"

"Yes, exactly, yes Sir."

Tabor looked at his watch and then said, "Okay, I'll consider a plea. What are you thinking?"

Sally took a deep breath and exhaled and asked, almost in a whisper, "Probation?"

His smile grew into a slow frown. "Good try, but no way. I will consider a light sentence, five years' time served and five years' probation." He looked at his watch again. "My offer is good for twenty-four hours, Miss Stevens. You can call me with your decision." He stood and extended his hand. As he held her hand and said, "Nine-thirty tomorrow morning will be twenty-four hours. Don't call me any later. Good luck to you Miss Stevens."

Sally thanked The District Attorney and left. She went directly to the courthouse public restroom and lost her breakfast.

CHAPTER

Sally knew she had to discuss the plea agreement the DA had offered as soon as possible. She went directly to the county jail and asked to meet with her client. It was ten thirty when she arrived and she was still feeling the effects of her upset stomach. As she waited in the holding room, she hoped that Agnes would be agreeable to the plea agreement. She knew the trial would be dramatic with such a famous person like Middy Adams. She knew with her limited experience that it would be impossible to win. Just then, Agnes came in, escorted by a lady jail attendant.

Sally stood and extended her hand to Agnes. Agnes reluctantly took her hand and gave Sally a forced smile and said, "You're back already?"

Sally wanted to appear excited and confident. "Yes, Agnes and I have some good news for you."

"I don't suppose they are dropping the charges, right?"

Sally looked away and then down at her note pad. "No, it's not that good, but the district attorney is offering a plea agreement of five years' time served and five years' probation."

Agnes was staring at Sally. "Well, I guess that is better than taking my chances at trial. Do you think so?"

This is what Sally was hoping to hear. She looked into Agnes' eyes and said, "I think this is best and I do hope you will accept it."

"So, is there any chance that the charges could still be dropped if a do accept the plea agreement?"

"No, I'm afraid not. We will have to appear before a judge with someone from the district attorney's office and the judge will ask if both parties are in agreement with the plea and then declare it final."

"But judges do have the power to change agreements and actually drop the charges. I see that all the time on Law and Order on TV."

Agnes, this is not TV or Law and Order. This is the real world. I'm sorry, but I can't see that happening."

"But it's not impossible."

Sally hesitated and then exhaled and said in a whisper, "No, it's not impossible. Now, I need to know if you accept this plea agreement. I do have to call the district attorney before nine-thirty tomorrow morning and give him our answer."

Agnes closed her eyes and bowed her head. Sally thought she might be praying and gave her the quiet moment she seemed to need. After at least a full minute, Agnes looked up and said, "I'll have my answer this afternoon. I need some time. Can you come back this afternoon?"

Sally knew this had to be a very difficult decision for Agnes and said, "Sure, how about three this afternoon. Will that be okay?"

Agnes only nodded and looked so sad.

Sally could not resist the urge to give Agnes a hug. She walked around the table that separated them and they held each other for a long moment. They both left the room from opposite doors without saying another word.

Sally had to retrieve her personal items from the front desk, including her cell phone. As she opened her phone, she saw one voice mail on the display. She pushed the key to call and heard a message from the district attorney's office. It was the receptionist she had met earlier that morning asking her to call her as soon as possible. She immediately called and again felt sick to her stomach. Why would they be calling her back so soon? Has the DA withdrawn his agreement? Then, she heard the receptionist's voice, "District Attorney's Office, may I help you."

Sally was just outside the county jail holding her cell tight against her ear. "Yes, this is Sally Stevens…you called for me earlier…I'm returning your call."

"Yes, Miss Stevens. Please hold for Mr. Tabor."

She was on hold for no more than fifteen seconds, but it seemed like an eternity. Then, she heard the click and Charles Tabor's voice. "Miss Stevens thanks for returning my call. Have you talked with your client yet?"

Sally thought the worst as she said, "Yes Sir. I just left her…"

"Did Miss Barnes accept the plea agreement?"

Sally hesitated and then said, "Well no, not yet. Has there been a change in the plea agreement?"

Tabor could hear the quiver in her voice. "Well yes, but it should be better for your client. I'm sure you haven't heard the news yet?"

"No Sir, what news?"

"Jimmy Skaggs hanged himself this morning in his jail cell."

"Oh, God…how terrible."

"Yes, it is and I'm sorry that he has taken his life, but we need to meet and talk about the charges against Miss Barnes. Can you come to my office now?"

"Yes Sir. I can be there in twenty minutes."

Sally was on her way to meet with the district attorney for the second time that morning.

When Sally entered the District Attorney waiting area, Charlie Tabor was there talking with his receptionist. He looked at Sally and said, "Well, when you said twenty minutes you must have meant ten. Please come in."

Sally followed Tabor into his office and stood. He sat down and pointed at the same chair she had sat in earlier that morning. "Please sit, we need to talk."

Sally sat and waited. He was looking at her with a different expression than he had at their first meeting.

He put his glasses on and took a document from his desk drawer and said, "This is my plea agreement and I was ready to sigh it if you had called with your client's agreement." He glanced at it and then placed it on his desk and removed his glasses. "So, she hasn't decided yet?"

Sally shook her head and said, "Not yet, she wants some time to think, she wants until this afternoon." She paused and then said, "I know you called me to talk about Jimmy Skaggs, right?"

He was still looking strange and she could not tell if he was happy or angry. But then he smiled and said, "Yes that's what I want to talk with you about. Do you think his death will make any difference on my offer to your client?"

She hesitated and then said, "No Sir. I don't think it would have any effect on your decision, but…"

"But what Miss Stevens?"

"Well, if I may speak freely, Sir."

He only nodded and again smiled.

She took a deep breath and exhaled as she always did when she was nervous. "The trial will be compromised without Jimmy Skaggs testimony."

He smiled again this time showing a lot of teeth. "So, are you willing to take this case to trial, thinking the judge will throw it out because of lack of evidence?"

"That's what I'm thinking right now, Sir."

"Well, Miss Stevens, it's my job to bring criminals to justice in this county, but I also have a reputation to maintain. I do not want this office to be embarrassed because of lack of proof, and with Jimmy Skaggs out of the picture, we would look pretty foolish. It would all be hearsay."

Sally was smiling now. "Are you telling me that you are going to request the charges be dismissed?"

"Miss Stevens, I am, but I wanted to hear you say that you would at least consider going to trial, with Jimmy Skaggs being unavailable." He stood and walked around his desk and extended his hand. She stood and took his. "We will have to appear before the judge, with your client and request the dismissal."

"And the judge will dismiss the charges, you're sure?"

"Yes, and you can tell your client today, that tomorrow she will be a free woman." He walked her to the door and said, "My office will call you with the court time for tomorrow, and one more thing."

"Yes?"

"Someday several years from now I hope you will

remember this case and the District Attorney who was impressed with your courage so early in your career."

She didn't want to be emotional but couldn't help it. With tears in her eyes she said, "I will always remember this day and the honor of getting to meet you. Thank you so much."

Sally left and headed back to the county jail to share the good news with Agnes Barnes.

CHAPTER

Agnes could not believe the guard when she said her lawyer was there again so soon. She wondered why she was coming back now when she had asked her to come back at three. She followed the guard to the holding room and saw Sally standing in the middle of the floor and smiling from ear to ear.

The guard left and Sally walked to Agnes and put her arms around her. Agnes was shocked and stood rigid, not returning the embrace.

"Sally, what's going on? Why are you back here so soon?"

"Oh, Agnes, I have great news." She kissed Agnes on the cheek, stood back, and then said, "You're going to be a free woman."

Agnes opened her mouth and finally said, "Free, you mean I'm getting out of here? What in the world is going on?"

They were now holding hands and smiling at each other. "Well, it's good news for you, but not good news for Jimmy Skaggs."

"He's not going to be released?"

Sally looked down at the floor and then back into Agnes's eyes and said, "Jimmy is dead, Agnes."

"Dead?"

"He hanged himself in his jail cell and that's the sad news, but because he will not be able to testify, the DA is dropping the charges against you. He feels they would not have a chance in court." She paused and then continued, "I'm so happy it happened before we could accept the plea agreement. The timing was perfect. I'm so happy for you, Agnes."

Agnes didn't know what to say. It was certainly good news for her, but she couldn't help but feel sorry for Jimmy. She hugged Sally then and gave her a kiss on the cheek. "Thank you so much."

Sally returned the kiss and continued to keep a firm embrace. "You're so welcome, Agnes. I think you are a very sweet person, and I love being with you." She then stood back and said, "We have to appear before a judge in the morning, and then you will be free."

Oh, Sally, I'm so glad you took my case. I know you took it as like you say, Free Bono."

Sally laughed and said, "Its Pro Bono, but yes I took it for no pay, but you could do something for me, if you will."

"How could I refuse you? You've saved my life, Sally. "You just name it and if I can, I will."

Sally smiled and leaned in closer and said in a whisper, "Stay with me tomorrow night."

"Stay with you? You mean, spend the night?"

"It would mean a lot to me. This is my first case and with this win, so to speak, I'd love to discuss it with you and have a nice evening together. Please think about it and let me know in the morning."

Agnes placed her hand on Sally's shoulder and said, "Okay, in the morning. Thanks again." She wondered why

Sally seemed so interested in her. Sally knew that Agnes was gay, could that be it? She was too exhausted to think and felt she must be overreacting.

Sally left the holding room more excited than she could ever remember. She knew what she wanted and hoped that Agnes knew also. Sally knew that Agnes and Patsy Holt were history and felt that Agnes needed someone in her life now to love her, and she wanted to be that person.

CHAPTER

Patsy had just heard about Jimmy Skaggs on the morning news and was about to let Middy know. She had kept Middy away from the news on TV, newspapers and radio for fear that too much would be about her. Now, she had to tell her about Jimmy. It was only fair as she would eventually find out and Patsy knew Middy should hear it from her.

To Patsy's surprise, she found Middy in the den, talking with her new *friend,* Beth Hatcher. They were both smiling and sitting very close to each other on the couch. When she walked into the room, Middy and Beth stopped talking and looked at her.

Beth smiled and said, "Well, come in and join us Patsy. We were just talking about the only time we met. It was over six years ago in Junction City, Kansas."

Patsy was afraid that too much had been said and hoped she was wrong. She knew Middy had feelings for Beth, knowing that she was actually her half-sister. She looked at Beth and smiled and then said, "Middy, I need to talk with you… in private."

Middy looked at Beth and then back at Patsy before saying, "in private?"

"Yes, Middy, please come with me." Patsy was frowning at Middy and again, hoping she hadn't said too much to Beth.

Middy slowly got up and said, "Excuse me, Beth; my manager wants to talk with me in private. Please keep your seat, I'll be right back and we can continue our conversation."

Patsy couldn't remember ever being upset with Middy. They had always agreed and never argued about anything. But this was different, Middy was not thinking clearly and Patsy was totally upset with her best friend.

As they both walked into the guest bedroom Patsy unloaded. "Middy Adams, what are you thinking? We both know who this girl is, but she never needs to know that she is your half-sister, Middy"

Middy turned to face Patsy and said, "Just when have you become the boss of my life?"

Patsy couldn't believe they were actually having this discussion. They loved each other but were now having more cross words. "Oh, Middy, please listen to me. No one loves you more than I do. I'm just trying to keep this from being a problem for you… for us." She paused and then said, "I have some important news to share with you."

"More important than trying to control my life?"

They were facing each other and looking into each other's eyes. Patsy closed her eyes and said in a whisper, "Jimmy Skaggs killed himself."

Middy was speechless. They both stood in complete silence and Middy slowly put her arms around Patsy and held her close. They both sobbed.

They slowly broke the embrace and stood back, holding hands, like they always had done since they first met. Then

Middy said, "Patsy, first of all, I'm sorry to hear about Jimmy. Is that all you know about his death?"

"Yes, it was on the news and that was all they said. I'm sure we will learn the details soon. I just didn't want you to hear it from any other source."

Middy was silent and she thought about the possibility of being pregnant and if she was, the father could never be located by her child like she had done. Too much had happened to Middy in the last several weeks. She just wanted to be alone and not have to have to think about anything. She smiled at Patsy and said, "Thanks for telling me. I know you love me and want what is best for me. Now, I have a request and hope you'll understand."

Patsy frowned and said, "You know I'll understand you've been through so much honey, what is it?"

"I just need to be alone a while, no conversation, no outside influence of any kind."

"You do mean alone here, right?"

"Oh yes, I want my bedroom upstairs. I have everything I need up there and I do need some quite time, time alone."

Patsy wasn't sure if it was a good idea for her being in the room where she had been attacked but wanted her to feel at ease and relaxed. "Middy, if you are sure about being up there."

Middy kissed her on the cheek and said, "I'm sure, so let's move Beth downstairs. Will you tell her?"

Patsy wasn't sure why Middy didn't want to tell her, but hoped it was because she had decided to limit her conversations with Beth. "I'll take care of it. You rest here and I'll let you know when your quarters are ready for you."

Middy sat on the bed and watched Patsy leave the room. She knew no one could begin to understand all of the strange feelings she was having and now with Jimmy's death, it was just too much.

CHAPTER

The next morning at eight, Sally was at the county jail to pick up her client for the hearing that was scheduled for ten. Agnes was excited and happy to see Sally arrive so early. They met again in the holding room and embraced. Agnes didn't want to admit it to herself, but she did feel comfort being with Sally.

The judge's office had sent an order for Agnes' release and Sally was given a copy when she had entered the jail. She showed the document to Agnes and smiled, "This is your ticket out of here."

"Oh Sally, I'm so happy and can't tell you how much I appreciate what you have done for me."

Sally thought to herself that she really hadn't done anything, it was the death of Jimmy Skaggs that was going to set her free, but she did want to take a little credit as she said, "That's my job and I'm happy to help you." She paused and then said, "Jimmy Skaggs death played a big part in your release, however."

At ten sharp they both stood before the circuit judge along with an assistant district attorney and heard the words they both wanted to hear from the judge. It was simple and Agnes was a free woman and all charges had been dismissed by the district attorney's office, and now the judge had made it official.

As they walked out of the justice center, Sally said, "My car is just across the street."

As they both sat in the car, Agnes said, "Are you taking me home, Sally?"

Sally smiled and said, "Have you thought about what I asked you yesterday?"

"Yes, and I really need to go home. We can talk some there and discuss the case like you said. I do need to get home and clean up and just take it easy for a while."

Sally started the car and said, "I understand completely, now do you need anything? May I stop at a store on the way and pick up something, milk, bread?"

They did stop at a convenience store and Agnes picked up a few items she knew she needed and then they went to the condo that Agnes and Patsy Holt had shared until Middy's attack.

Sally was impressed with the condo and walked into each room, commenting on how nice it was. She knew that Agnes wanted to clean up and rest. After Agnes had put up the few items they had brought in, Sally said, "Why don't you go shower and clean up and I'll make us a sandwich."

Agnes felt strange with Sally being there and even more so, with her wanting to stay and visit, but again, she felt she owed her that much for all she had done for her. She went to the bathroom and left Sally in the kitchen.

When Agnes returned, Sally was sitting at the small kitchen table, with a cup of coffee in her hand. "You sure look better and I'm sure you must feel better, Agnes."

Agnes smiled and said, "I felt so dirty in that jail cell. I hope I never have to see one again."

Sally sat her coffee on the table and stood up and walked to Agnes. She put her hands on her shoulders and said, "I would never let that happen to you again, Agnes."

Agnes had thought that Sally was gay from her actions when they first met, and now she was sure. Sally was smiling and starting to put her arms around Agnes. She had to stop this before it went too far as she said, "Sally, I'm sure you think that I am gay…and well, I am, but I'm not looking for, nor do I want to have a sexual relationship with anyone. Please stop this. I really do appreciate what you've done for me, but I'm not interested in having a relationship with you."

Sally dropped her hands to her side and took a step back and said, "Well, I guess I'm not rich enough for you, Miss Barnes. I really felt that we had something for each other, but I guess I was wrong."

Agnes couldn't deny being gay, but this made her feel cheap. Being approached by a stranger made her feel like a cheap whore. She slowly moved close to Sally and placed her hand on her shoulder and said, Sally, I know you want someone to love and be with you, a lover, and a partner for life. Believe me, I've had that desire and thought I had it with Patsy Holt." She stood back from Sally and looked toward the door and then said, "I really need you to leave, Sally. We are not meant to be together, but like I said, you will find someone, and I hope it will be for a lifetime. I have nothing against you and will always remember how you helped me get through this difficult time in my life."

Sally walked to the door without making eye contact with Agnes and stopped. Without turning to look at Agnes she said, "I am leaving, but I will always think we were meant to be that special couple, but now we'll never know."

Agnes watched as Sally walked out the door without another word.

Agnes knew she had to see Patsy before leaving Nashville. Patsy had caused all of these problems and she needed to pay, and Agnes intended to make her pay.

46

CHAPTER

Later that morning, the local news was all about Jimmy Skaggs committing suicide and the charges against Agnes Barnes being dismissed. Middy and Patsy had watched the morning news and were both shocked about Agnes being released.

Beth soon appeared and as usual all smiles. "Good Morning, Ladies." She went directly to Middy and started to check her vital signs.

Middy smiled at her and said, "This is just like the hospital, a nurse checking to see if I am okay."

"Well, I'm sure you are okay, but for the rest of this week, we'll keep a check."

Patsy really didn't like being present when Beth was with Middy and made an excuse that she was going to check out Middy's quarters upstairs and left them alone.

Middy knew Patsy was worried that she was going to tell Beth about their relationship, but she had no intention of telling her. After Beth had recorded all of Middy's vital signs, Middy said, "So, I know that Patsy has told you that I want to move back to my quarters."

"Yes, and I think you'll be fine back up there. I am glad to see you wanting to get back to a normal life, Middy."

Middy thought, I'm not sure if a normal life is in the cards for me. "Well, thanks, Beth. I'm sure going to try my best to get back."

Beth smiled and looked at Middy with her strange eyes. Middy couldn't get Bill Hatcher out of her mind, especially now, knowing that he had died only six months ago. She wondered how he had died and finally said, "Was you father sick? I mean, did he have health problems…before he died?"

Beth's smile was replaced with a frown as she said, "No, he wasn't sick." She turned away from Middy and said, "It was a car wreck."

Middy stared at Beth and then said, "You mean he was killed in his car?"

"It was his car, but he was not driving." Beth looked away then back to look into Middy's eyes. "It was my mother, she killed him." She covered her face with both hands and sobbed.

"So, it was an accident, right?"

"Yes, it was an accident, but my mother is a terrible driver. My dad always drove, but that time she had the car and picked him up from work and ran a stop sign. I know she did not mean to kill him, but her reckless driving did kill him." Beth continued to cry and then stood up and said, "I'm supposed to be helping you and I'm causing you to feel sorry for me." She hesitated and then continued with, "I'm so sorry to be so unprofessional. Please forgive me."

Middy wasn't sure how to respond to Beth. She did want to comfort her as she would anyone after hearing about them losing their dad. "I'm so sorry you lost your dad and I can only imagine the shock of losing him." She reached for Beth's hand and held it firmly. "Please don't feel unprofessional about telling me about your loss. I think you are a very kind and loving person and if I can, in any way, be of comfort to you, it will be the least I can do."

Middy stood and they embraced, both feeling very sad, Beth with a loss of a loved one and Middy only feeling sorry for Beth's loss. He had been her dad also, but she had no feelings for him.

Patsy returned to find them locked in their embrace. She stood with her arms crossed, again hoping Middy hadn't given in to the temptation she knew she had.

CHAPTER

The three ladies had a quiet dinner and made small talk about current events and avoided the subject of Jimmy Skaggs. Beth offered to clean up the dishes and put the food away, but Patsy insisted on doing that chore. It was obvious to Beth that Patsy wanted some private time with Middy, so she excused herself and went to the guest bedroom, closing the door behind her.

Middy and Patsy went upstairs after getting the downstairs kitchen in order. They sat at the small kitchen table they had sat at over the years. They had had many conversations and many discussions about future tours and plans for their future together at this small table. This time, the subject matter was totally different. Patsy wanted to get Middy's attention and hopefully make her understand how devastating their lives would be if Beth ever found out the truth.

Patsy reached for Middy's hands as always and held then softly and said, "Now, I want this to be my time to talk and I know you'll listen and give me this time."

Middy said, "You know I'll listen, but first, I need to tell you how Bill Hatcher died." She then told her about the car accident and how Beth had felt about her mother. She then became quiet and waited for Patsy.

Middy looked so different to Patsy. She realized that she had been traumatized by the attack and learning about Jimmy's and her own father's death. Not to mention the possibility of being pregnant with Jimmy Skaggs' baby. She wanted to comfort Middy and hopefully reach her on some level to help her heal first of all, but right now, she wanted her to get Beth Hatcher out of her system. She was so afraid that Middy had already made up her mind to tell Beth the truth.

So, she began with, "Honey, we are at a crossroads in our lives. I don't want to repeat all of the things I've said about neglecting you and causing us to be where we are now. We've had that discussion and I know you have forgiven me, so that's all I'm going to say about our relationship."

Middy tried to smile but kept that different look in her eyes. She looked at Patsy and then down at the table and said, "I know what you are concerned about, and I'll listen and then it will be my turn, okay?"

Patsy knew she had to make her best effort to convince her. "We need to realize what kind of an impact this could have on Beth. We know that she adored her father and wanted to please him by becoming a registered nurse. She has achieved this goal and I think is a very good and professional nurse. She will get over her father's death in time. I know she will never forget him and always wonder why he had to die, but in time, she will learn to live with it." Patsy sat up straight in her chair and pointed her index finger directly at Middy and said, "Now, Middy, do you think she would ever feel the same about the father, the father she loved and admired so much, knowing that he raped an innocent mentally ill young woman."

Patsy again sat back in her chair and stared at Middy, waiting for her to respond.

Middy got up and went to the sink and filled a glass with water and came back and sat down. She took a sip and then looked over the glass at Patsy and said, "So, what you are saying, this isn't all about me or my feelings. Am I right?"

"Exactly."

Middy sat in total silence and closed her eyes.

Middy and Patsy kept their cell phones within reach at all times. Both phones were on the small kitchen table in front of them. They had the same type phones and many times picked up the wrong phone after hearing one ring. They both stared at the display as Patsy's phone vibrated and began to ring. It was Agnes Barnes' picture and number.

Middy looked at Patsy and said, "Well, are you going to answer it?"

Patsy shook her head and said, "No, why should I talk with her?"

"Well, it might be the right time to put an end to your relationship. That is if you really want to end it."

Patsy was furious as she snatched the phone while glaring at Middy and said, "What do you want Agnes?" Patsy waited and could hear Agnes breathing in the phone.

Her voice was softer than usual as she finally said, "Patsy, I'm sorry you hate me." She paused and started crying. After her pause she said, "I just want to talk with you one more time before I leave. Is that too much to ask, after we have meant so much to each other?"

Patsy was sure that Agnes was involved with Middy's

attack and found it hard to talk with her, but finally said, "So, what do you want to say to me?"

"I want to see you and talk…please listens. I'll meet you anywhere you say, I just need to have closure and seeing you one more time will give me closure. Please… Please."

Patsy looked at Middy as she covered her cell phone with her hand. "She wants to meet with me. She said this would be closure for her."

"You're asking me, Patsy? She's your friend, or should I say old lover?"

"Why are you acting like this, Middy? I've told you that it's over between Agnes and me."

Middy stood, pick up her cell and walked into her bedroom and closed the door.

Patsy couldn't believe how Middy was acting. She knew she was upset with her about Beth and maybe this was the reason she was being so unreasonable about Agnes. Patsy's heart was pounding as she took her hand off her cell and pressed it against her ear. She took a deep breath and exhaled. "Where do you want to meet, Agnes?"

CHAPTER

Patsy couldn't believe she was actually going to meet Agnes Barnes, but she was driving north on I-65 toward Nashville and the condo she and Agnes had shared. Agnes had requested the meeting at their former home to ensure privacy and in her mind, hopefully, rekindle a love they had both shared. She knew Patsy thought she had control of Jimmy Skaggs and had been the person to convince him to attack Middy. Now, with Jimmy dead, no one would ever be able to confirm her involvement in Middy's attack. Agnes truly wanted Middy out of her and Patsy's lives, and in her heart of hearts, still wished that Middy was gone...dead even.

Agnes was sitting on the sofa when she heard the key turn in the door. She smiled as Patsy walked in. Patsy was not smiling, but Agnes could tell that she had been crying from the red eyes she kept blinking.

Agnes stood and looked down and then back to meet Patsy's red eyes and said, "It's good to see you Patsy. How are you?"

Patsy's emotions were so confused, as she went from anger to sadness, and a little of the feeling of love for her former lover. She started to speak but sobbed and bowed her head.

Agnes took advantage of the situation and walked to Patsy and placed her hands on her shoulders and said, "You're the only person I ever loved and I miss you and need you so much."

Patsy pushed Agnes away and finally did speak. "What makes you think I could have any kind of love for you after what you and Jimmy did to Middy?"

Agnes cried and again tried to approach Patsy. Patsy wanted to slap her, but instead took her in her arms and held her as they sobbed.

Agnes' body was trembling and her voice was impossible to understand. She finally became quiet and said in a whisper, "You know I don't like Middy, but I could never do anything to hurt her, or anyone."

Patsy wanted to believe Agnes, but really could not. Could Jimmy Skaggs have done this awful thing on his own? Jimmy knew how much Middy and Agnes disliked each other and maybe, just maybe he did do it on his own. She decided to listen to Agnes and hoped she could convince her that she wasn't involved. They were still embraced as Patsy said, "Agnes, I want you to tell me what you knew or didn't know about Jimmy's actions."

Agnes released her embrace and stood back and spoke. "Oh, thank you, Patsy. That's what I want most of all. I want you to listen and please, try to believe me." She motioned toward the sofa and they both sat down as Agnes continued. "I did tell Jimmy how much I disliked Middy and how I thought she wanted you and me to be apart. I never, in anyway suggested that he harm Middy." She became silent and looked directly into Patsy's eyes, hoping she believed her.

Patsy sat looking back at Agnes, still wanting to believe

her. She had been in love with Agnes and at one time thought she would spend the rest of her life with her. Now she was with her, like they had been when they were lovers. She still had feelings for Agnes, but she had made a commitment to God and to herself to devote her life to Middy. She knew Middy would not have been subjected to such a horrible attack if she had been there to protect her. So, how could she even think about getting back with Agnes Barnes?

Agnes knew from Patsy's expression that she didn't believe her story. She had expected this and wasn't surprised, but it still hurt. She had really been in love with Patsy and like Patsy, thought they would be lifetime lovers. She did have a plan B and it was time to use it. She got up and walked a few steps and turned and pointed her index finger at Patsy.

Patsy stared at her and then said, "What's this? Are you going to attack *me* now?

Agnes's look was one Patsy had never seen before. Her eyes were glaring and her mouth was twisted and showing her teeth. She kept her finger pointing at Patsy and then spoke in a very harsh voice. "You've destroyed my life and used me like a cheap whore. I really loved you Patsy Holt, but now I have only hatred for you and your precious Middy Adams. I hope you both have a miserable life and live to be old ugly women." She paused again and walked within a foot of Patsy and placed her finger within an inch of her nose. "I want money...you owe me, and you and your wonderful partner have lots of it." Patsy slapped her hand and said, "You get out of my face and shut your bitchy mouth. I owe you nothing. I didn't force you to have a love affair with me, Agnes. You are just as gay as I am and welcomed me into your life. And one more thing, you are the person who caused this breakup, you and little Jimmy Skaggs." She paused and cried briefly and then continued. "Just in case you're wondering, I don't believe a word you just told me. I am sure you used Jimmy to get rid of Middy, but she's safe now and I will give my life if necessary, to keep her safe for the rest of her life."

Agnes was holding her hand from the slap Patsy had given her. She then put her hands on her hips and said, "No one can ever prove that I was involved in Middy's attack and I really don't care what you believe. I am a free woman and all charges have been dropped by a judge." She continued to glare at Patsy and continued,

"So, we both know our relationship is over, but I still want money. You owe me, Patsy."

Patsy closed her eyes and then asked, "How much?"

They were both silent for a long moment and Agnes said in a whisper, "A million. I want a million dollars."

Patsy's voice was a whisper also as she said, "I won't do a million, but will transfer five hundred thousand to your bank account…and I will also transfer the deed to our condo to you."

This was more than Agnes had expected. She smiled at Patsy one last time and walked out of the room.

Patsy went to her car and drove back south, hopefully to continue her life with Middy. Her next concern was the relationship Middy was having with Beth. She now had Agnes Barnes out of their lives and knew Beth would be her next challenge.

CHAPTER 49

Middy and Beth had talked the entire time Patsy had been gone to meet with Agnes. Middy had been very open and honest with Beth regarding Patsy and Agnes. Beth had known about the couple, but had not had it confirmed by someone who knew firsthand. Beth was surprised how Middy had been so open and told her these very private things about her life with Patsy Holt.

Patsy arrived later and heard Middy and Beth as she opened the front door, they were upstairs talking. They soon became silent as they heard Patsy coming up the stairs. As she entered the kitchen, they both looked at her without a word.

Patsy broke the silence as she said, "Well, it's good to see you all also."

More silence and then Middy said, "So, Patsy, are you back? Are you going to live here with us?"

Patsy placed her purse on the small kitchen table and pulled out one of the chairs and sat down. She looked directly at Middy standing by the kitchen sink, and then at Beth and said, "You are asking if I am going to live here with us, both of you?"

Middy slowly walked to the table and sat across from

Patsy. Her expression was one of concern as she frowned at Patsy and then said, "Patsy, you and I have been closer than most people. I have wanted our relationship to continue and even grow stronger with time, but now I'm not sure if you want this life with me."

Patsy felt like she was going to be sick. This was more than she could handle. After everything Middy had been through and Patsy feeling so responsible for what had happened, it was too much. She slowly stood up and reached for her purse, knocking it off the table. As she bent over to retrieve it, she fell to her knees and vomited.

Beth immediately came to her aid and moved her away from the vomit, placing her hand on Patsy's forehead. Middy had not moved and continued sat and stare at Patsy. Beth, being a nurse was there without a second thought. She wasn't surprised by Middy' lack of concern as she understood the trauma and fear Middy had lived with over the past weeks. Beth knew Middy needed someone in her life and with the possibility of Patsy not being that person, made her more afraid and angrier. Beth knew these two ladies were meant to be together and she planned to help them reunite if possible.

Beth looked up, still holding Patsy's head and said, "Middy, would you get a cool wet washcloth for us?"

Middy slowly got up and went to the kitchen sink and ran water over a dirty washcloth and pitched it on the floor next to Beth and Patsy and then went to her bedroom without another word.

Beth turned her attention back to Patsy and ignored the dirty washcloth and helped her to her feet. She then took a paper napkin from the table and wiped Patsy's face and then said, "Let me help you to your room."

Patsy held Beth's hand as they descended the steps to the first floor. Beth took her to her bathroom and helped her clean her face with a clean wet washcloth. Patsy assured her that she was okay, and then Beth went back upstairs and cleaned up the vomit from the kitchen floor.

Patsy was still in her bedroom and was lying down when Beth came back downstairs. She was surprised to see Beth entering her room. Beth stood at the foot of her bed and said, "I'm so sorry this is happening, Patsy. I would really like to talk with you, if you will allow me."

Patsy couldn't imagine what she possibly could want to talk about but agreed as she slowly sat up on the side of her bed.

Beth sat across from her on the dressing table chair and began. "Patsy, I know you must think of me as a threat to your relationship with Middy. I want you to know that I have no intentions of coming between you two." She paused and looked down at the floor then back to meet Patsy's eyes. "I know you realize more than anyone, how this attack on Middy has affected her life and causes her to have doubts about your commitment to her. Many times, brain injuries can have a lasting effect on a person, but with time people usually get back to their normal self." She looked at Patsy, hoping she was understanding what she was saying, and then continued. "I've only known the kind of love you and Middy share once in my life, and it was with my father. He was my father and everyone should love their parents, but my love for him was more than a father and daughter. He was my inspiration; the person who always gave me encouragement when I needed it. As I've said before, he's the reason I am a nurse and without his involvement, I would never have gone to nursing school and never been a nurse. Now, I am telling you this to let you know that I understand, completely how much you and Middy mean to each other. I know you are the reason Middy is where she is today." She paused again and closed her eyes for a long moment, then opened her eyes and placed her hand on Patsy's and continued. "There should never be anyone or anything to come between two people who mean so much to each other as you and Middy Adams. As Middy has always said, you are a team, a true partnership."

Patsy was sitting with her eyes wide open and her mouth agape and finally said, "So, are you saying that you are not moving in here with Middy?"

Beth released her hand and smiled as tears filled her eyes. "Patsy, I'm sure a lot of people wouldn't hesitate to take advantage of an opportunity to spend their life with a super star like Middy Adams. She has asked me to stay with her and give her support and love that she needs so much, but that support and love is already assigned to her closest and dearest friend, and we both know who that is, right?"

Patsy was crying then as she stood up and opened her arms to Beth. Beth stood also and they embraced. Patsy spoke softly as she held Beth close. "So, what are you going to do?"

Beth stood back and looked toward the doorway and then back at Patsy and said, "Well the first thing I'm going to do is go upstairs and tell Middy the same thing I've just told you including how blessed she is to have you in her life, and then I'm packing my bags and going back to

Vanderbilt Medical Center, where I belong. I am a nurse and a dedicated one, and my life will be there helping people like my father encouraged me to do."

Patsy watched as Beth walked out the door, heading for the stairs. She was still very upset, but wanted to believe things were going to be all right with her and Middy.

It took longer than Patsy thought, but thirty minutes later, Beth and Middy walked into her room. They were both smiling and both had tears in their eyes.

Middy walked directly to Patsy and kissed her on the cheek and said, "Beth has opened my eyes to what I should have known all along, Patsy." She looked back at Beth and then continued. "We are truly blessed to have found each other. It's not only my success because of your encouragement; it's a very special relationship that was meant to be. If I am never able to sing again or entertain anyone, I will always love you and be thankful that we found each other."

Patsy couldn't speak as she held Middy and sobbed. It was a long time before they broke their embrace, and when they did, they both looked around the room for Beth, but she was gone. They both knew this was the best for them and Beth.

Patsy knew Middy would always remember Beth and her father William Hatcher's death. He was Middy's father also…and Beth would always be her sister. She could only hope and pray that Middy could accept this and go on with her life. Patsy knew she had been given a second chance to restore a love that few people could only imagine. This was truly a renewal of their lives, and they both were so relieved to be together again and totally committed to each other.

50

CHAPTER

Rick Stone had learned that Middy was out of danger after she had been in the hospital for a week, and knew he must get back to Topeka and hopefully convince his future wife that he still loved her and wanted her. He knew it was going to be difficult, knowing how much Jenny disliked Middy Adams; in fact, he was sure Jenny must hate her now after all she had to endure. He had booked a flight from Nashville to Topeka Saturday morning and was now at the airport with over two hours to wait for his flight. He had called Jenny's cell several times, each time leaving a message telling her he was coming home, home to be with her. She had not answered any of the calls or returned his voice mail messages.

When Rick finally arrived home, his mailbox was full and he had a package on his front porch. He took the mail and package inside and put it and the mail on his kitchen table. He couldn't imagine what could be in the package, as it had no return address. He peeled the tape off the top and opened it and the first thing he saw was a note, handwritten on an index card. It was Jenny's handwriting. The note was brief and only contained a few words on two lines. Tears filled his eyes as he read it softly aloud to himself. "Rick, please don't try to contact me. Our life is over and I never want to see you again as long as I live." Under the note were several love letters he had written to her over the past year and a copy of their wedding announcement from the local newspaper. Her engagement ring was taped to the bottom of the announcement.

Rick sat down hard and put his head on the table and cried. His first marriage had been a mistake and ended bitterly as they both had realized they were not meant to be together.

After a few moments, his cell phone rang and he thought, maybe, it could be her. As he looked at the phone, he noticed there was no number and decided it must be a scam call and canceled the call. After a few more seconds, his voice mail sound buzzed. He opened the voice mail and heard a very soft voice. "Rick, this is Middy. I know you are upset with me after all you have been through. I know your girlfriend, future wife, is upset from what you told me. I need to talk with you and hope you will call me back. I need to tell you how sorry I am. So, please call me. I am giving you my unlisted cell number and hope I can hear from you." She then gave him the number and the voice mail ended.

Rick stared at his phone and thought about calling her but couldn't think of anything to say at that moment. He was to upset with Jenny's note and knowing he was losing his bride-to-be. He knew all of this was because of Middy Adams and her controlling attitude. Well, he had her private number and could call her, but really didn't want to and decided not to call.

Saturday night and Sunday were some of the worst times he had spent in his life. He couldn't sleep and spent most of the time crying and trying to think about his future and what he could do to get through this awful time. He knew he had a great position with Vital Statistics and had to get back to some kind of a normal life.

He was ashamed of his actions after reading Jenny's note, saying she never wanted to see him. He had broken some dishes and trashed the kitchen in a total fit of anger. He knew he would have to clean it up later.

CHAPTER

Sunday morning, back in Franklin, Tennessee, Middy was crying and continuing to look at her cell phone. Patsy was up and thought she could hear sobs from upstairs. She quickly went upstairs and found Middy sitting at her small dining table with tear filled eyes.

"Honey, what in in world is wrong? Are you feeling bad, does anything hurt?"

Middy looked up at her best friend and said, "I am so upset with what I've done to Rick Stone. I called his cell yesterday and left him a message. I told him how sorry I was and left him my private number. I told him I need to talk with him, but he has not called back. Oh, Patsy I am so upset. How can I get him to talk with me?" I am concerned that his visit with me has caused his future wife to be upset. He lost his first wife and now, I may cause him to lose this one."

Patsy went to her an sat next to her and placed her hand on her shoulder. "Middy, you have tried. He should be man enough to at least talk with you."

Patsy sat for a few moments and finally said, "Middy, I have an idea. Maybe, just maybe I can call his girlfriend, Jenny, I think that is her name."

"Call her, what do you mean?

"Now, Middy you know I want to help, so trust me. I have an idea and it could work."

Middy looked at Patsy and smiled. "Honey, you are always there for me and you know I do trust you. Will you call her soon?"

Patsy stood up and looked down at Middy. "It is Sunday, maybe I can find her today."

Middy continued to smile as Patsy left and went downstairs.

CHAPTER

Rick Stone was up on Monday morning and knew he had to get back to his office. He had a very important position with the state of Kansas, being the Director of Vital Statistics. It was the job he had wanted from his first day with the agency. But now, his life was going to be different and totally changed from what it was just a week ago. It was true that he still had his dream job, but the love of his life had told him that she never wanted to see him again. He wanted his Jenny back most of all. Now, he sat and had a single cup of coffee and looked around his trashed kitchen. He was actually ashamed of his behavior, trashing his kitchen. It was a total mess and he knew it must be cleaned up and get some kind of life back. He stood and finished his cup and looked around the mess and then went out the door. Driving to work, he knew his employees and especially his secretary would be asking about is upcoming wedding. They knew he had taken the week off to be with Jenny and make final wedding plans. Hopefully none of his involvement with Middy had made the local news. Her attack had been national news, but he had not seen anything that had mentioned his name. The obvious people like Jimmy Skaggs and Agnes Barnes were named because of their arrest after her attack.

Kathy Crane, his secretary met him at his office door and gave him a hug and said, "Oh, Rick, it's so great to have you back. We have all been thinking about what a wonderful week you and Jenny were having, planning your wedding."

Rick smiled and said, "Thank you, Kathy." He looked around the general office area and saw no other employees. It was only 7:30 and most arrived at 8:00. Kathy had always arrived early to have mail and calls that came in during the night ready for Rick. He smiled again and said, "I appreciate everyone thinking about me. I do have a request of you."

Kathy looked puzzled as she said, "What is it, Rick?"

"After being gone for a week, I need time alone to catch up on paperwork and phone calls. Please let everyone know that I will not be available today."

Kathy wanted to ask why, why all day? But he was her boss and she always respected his request. She smiled again and said, "You won't be disturbed...welcome back."

Rick sat behind his desk and stared at the stack of mail, knowing he had to get his life back. He then thought about the phone and the possibility of Middy calling again. He pushed his intercom button and said, "Kathy, I also do not want to accept any phone calls today...from anyone."

"Yes sir," came over his intercom.

Kathy had worked with Rick from his very first day and they had been friends from the beginning. Early on in their careers they had dated a few times, once with a movie and dinner and a few other times, lunch off grounds at local fast-food restaurants. Their relationship had not developed and

Rick had married his first wife a few years after he first met Middy Adams. His marriage had not worked and he and his wife agreed they were not right for each other. He was a single man again and during his single years, was promoted to Director of the Vital Statistics Agency. That was when he met Jenny and felt he had found the love of his life. He had told her about meeting Middy Adams before and after she became a super star. He could tell then by her reaction that she had no interest in his past attractions to other women, including his ex-wife. He had almost told her about the few dates he had with Kathy Crane in the past. She was his secretary by then and he knew if he told Jenny, he would have to at least move her to another position or ask her to resign. So, he had kept his mouth shut about Kathy.

Kathy had always taken coffee to Rick each morning and was reluctant to but decided he surely wouldn't object to her entering his office. So, she did take the coffee in as she did on any normal day. She closed the door as he had said he want privacy. He immediately looked up when he heard the door close and frowned, but the frown was replaced with his warm smile as he saw it was Kathy.

Kathy smiled and said, "I hope I'm not upsetting you, Rick."

He knew she had no idea what had happened to him the past week. He sat back and pushed his chair back and said, "Kathy, I'm so sorry for being so cold and indifferent with you." He then moved some papers, making room for the coffee cup as she sat it down and looked into his eyes.

"Rick, we've known each other for a long time and I know you well enough to know when something is wrong. You know I have never asked you about your personal life, but I feel that something had to happen last week." She hesitated and then closed her eyes and said, "Are you and Jenny okay?"

She opened her eyes and saw that he was crying and shaking his head from side to side. She could not control her feelings for him and went around his desk and placed her hand on his back and said, "I'm sorry, Rick. I would never say or do anything to upset you; I'm just so worried about you. You have always been so special to me and you know I that I love you."

Rick turned in his chair and put his arms around Kathy and continued to cry. She was so glad there were no windows on the office side. His only window was behind his desk, looking outside. She stood with his arms around her waist and held his head against her belly. She knew he needed this comfort and was happy to be there for him in his time of need. It was several seconds before he released her and reached for her hands. As he held both of her hands in his he said, "Kathy, we have always been friends and you have always been very supportive to me." He looked up to meet her eyes and said, "I need to talk with you about my terrible week. I need to talk with someone and I hope you will humor me."

She knew he must have had a bad time with Jenny. She really never liked Jenny and wondered why Rick was so taken with her. Kathy could see that Jenny was very controlling and had a totally different personality that Rick. Her jealousy was obvious to Kathy as she remembered how she would tell her when she called for Rick. She would always make it clear that he was her man and no one else's. She wondered if Jenny thought she was a competitor.

Kathy wanted to hear what Rick wanted to tell her as she said, "Rick, I'm here for you. Please feel free to tell me anything. I do want to comfort you."

He continued to look at her with his eyes full of tears. He released her hands and said, "Please sit for a moment."

Kathy sat in the chair next to his desk where she had taken dictation so many times and continued to look into his watery eyes.

"First of all, my week is totally unbelievable and would take more time that we have. I will tell you that it all started with Middy Adams."

"Middy Adams?" Kathy asked with a look of shock.

"Yes, you took her call and transferred her to me, remember?"

"Oh, yes, I will never forget her asking for you and finally telling me who she was. She has been your friend for a long time, right?"

Rick frowned and said, "Was, my friend, but no more." He looked down at his desk and shook his head.

Kathy wanted to help him but could not understand what Middy Adams could have possibly done to change the way he felt about her. Then she thought about Jenny and how jealous she was and said, "And Jenny was upset about the call?"

Rick knew Kathy was aware of Jenny's jealously. "Well yes, that, and a lot more." He hesitated again and said, "It is just too much to burden you with, Kathy. I'm just so upset about my current state of mind." He cried again and placed his head on his desk.

Kathy felt helpless and sat beside him and waited.

He finally stopped crying and looked at her and said,

"Can you believe that I have actually trashed my kitchen because of all of this. If you saw it you would think that I had gone crazy."

She again, had no idea how to respond and reached for his hand again and said, "Maybe we could talk after work. I want to help you get over this, whatever it is."

"Kathy, you are such a good friend and I do trust you. I really need to go home and clean up my mess. I really am not ready to be here yet." He hesitated again and then said, "I don't want to take advantage of our friendship and for sure not ask you to help me because I'm your boss."

"Oh Rick, you know I would never think that. Now, I can either come to your house, or you may come to my apartment after work and we can talk. You know I'm very concerned.

Rick could not speak as he smiled at her and nodded.

She knew he needed to be out of there and said, "Please go home and do what you need to do and then call me later and let me know where you want to meet. I do love you."

He watched her as she went out the door, after turning back to smile at him.

CHAPTER

Rick sat in his office after Kathy left, wondering if it was a good idea to meet with her. She had been his friend since their first day at Vital Statistics. It was strange how they started on the same day. She was in a pool of secretaries and he started in records, posting information and entering records in the computer. They had both worked at different levels and each level was a learning curve for both of them. They did see each other most days and usually in the cafeteria during lunch. Many times, they discussed their job duties and sometimes went off grounds and had lunch together. They did have a few dates, going to movies and dinner, but had never been serious about each other. Rick sat and smiled as he thought of the times they had worked in the same building, but not in the same department. Now, after over fifteen years, she was his secretary. He knew she cared for him and was truly concerned about his state of mind. He was also concerned and knew that having someone to share his concerns with would help him get through this crisis. He did feel guilty asking her to be his sounding board, but she had insisted that she wanted to help.

He stood and looked around the office, then picked up a stack of mail and placed it in his briefcase. He thought if he didn't feel like coming in tomorrow, he could at least catch up on some of his mail at home. He walked out and noticed that Kathy was not at her desk. He hesitated and then thought she was on a break or in the restroom. He left the building.

Kathy was in the lady's room, crying. She had been so upset seeing Rick in such an emotional state. She was actually worried that he might really have a mental breakdown and hoped she would be able to help him. She needed to be strong and give him her support and love. She had wondered over the years about his love for her. She could never see it, but had wondered if he had felt anything for her. She had seen him married to the wrong woman and now maybe losing another wrong woman in her opinion. She hoped he would be gone when she returned to her desk, and he was. She finished her reports for the day and decided to take off at noon. This had been an accepted practice when someone had finished the task for the day, but no one would be allowed to abuse this practice. She had taken off early very few times. She needed this time to prepare for Rick. She knew he had her cell and would call her as promised. She did leave at noon and stopped by the local grocery and bought frozen chicken pot pies, lettuce, tomatoes and carrots for a salad. She also picked up a cherry pie in the deli. She knew it was Rick's favorite.

Rick took a warm shower when he got home, even though he had showered that morning. He felt it would help him sleep. He then went to his bedroom and did sleep. He awoke three hours later and looked at the bedside clock. It was 2:15 P.M. and he was relieved. He wasn't sure if he had slept all evening. He decided to clean up his mess in the kitchen and then call Kathy. It took him a little over an hour to get the kitchen put back together. He threw away the broken dishes and took out the trash. He came back in and surveyed the kitchen and it looked fine. He thought he could call in a pizza and have Kathy meet him at his house. He called her to invite her over.

Kathy saw his name on her display and said, "Hi, Mr. Rick Stone."

He could not keep from smiling, just hearing her voice. "Well, this must be Miss Kathy Crane." He paused and then said, "I hope you still want to meet with me this evening."

"Yes, I do; in fact, I have all the good stuff to make us a good dinner."

He was surprised. "Well, I was going to have you over here and order a pizza. Are you sure you want to cook?"

"It's just chicken pot pie and a salad…and one of those cherry pies."

His mood was changing by the moment. "You have sold me, Miss Crane. What time should I arrive?"

She was smiling with tears in her eyes. "Could you be here, say at five?"

He was so touched by her kindness. "I'll be there and what can I bring?"

"Yourself, see you at five."

The call ended and Rick cried again. He left his house at 4:30 to be sure and not be late. He had never been to her apartment but did know where it was. She had told him the location in the past and he had seen the complex in passing. It was an up scaled complex and in a very nice neighborhood. He knew she lived in apartment 325 and went directly to the elevator and to the third floor. Her door was the last on the left and had a good view out the side window. He pushed the doorbell button and took a deep breath. This was going to be a first for both of them.

When she opened the door, he wasn't sure what he was feeling. It was happiness, excitement and most of all a pure feeling of peace. The peace he had missed in his life in the past week.

She was smiling as usual when she saw him. Then she frowned and said, "Uh, do you have an appointment, Sir?" She always asked that of people coming to see Rick at the office. They both laughed at her question.

Rick laughed for the first time since he had been home and said, "Yes, with Miss Crane."

She stood back and waved her arm to the inside and said, "Well, you must be Mr. Stone."

They shared a long hug and she whispered, "I'm so happy you are here, Rick."

He continued to hold her and said, "Me too."

They broke their embrace and Rick looked around the living room. It was very nice with modern furniture and a large flat screen TV, mounted on the wall. A large window at the end of the room gave a great view of the area around the complex.

She could see that he was impressed with her apartment and said, "Let me show you around. I found this about three years ago, well I told you then, do you remember?"

He was looking and nodding. "Yeah, I had no idea how nice it is. This is a nice place and a beautiful setting."

She was so pleased that he liked it. She felt like a kid showing her parents something new she had learned. They walked into the kitchen and then into the laundry room and finally into her bedroom. It was large also and had a walk-in closet and a full bath with a large glass enclosed shower and long vanity. They both stood in silence. She knew he was impressed.

"Well, what do you think, Rick?"

"I love it. I could live here. It has everything."

She thought to herself, I wish you did live here. Then, it would have everything for sure. She took his arm and said, "Well, I have wine. Would you like a glass before we devour that chicken pot pie?"

After they finished the wine, they had dinner and had a very casual conversation and she asked about the dinner and he agreed it was good but said the cherry pie was the best. They both laughed but knew it was time to talk about Rick's awful week.

Kathy brought a glass of wine for each of them and waited to hear his sad story. She sat with her mouth open as Rick finished his story of his unbelievable week. She could not believe how he could have survived after these terrible experiences. She could only imagine Rick being behind bars and treated like a common criminal, but most of all, how Jenny had treated him, her lover, and her future husband. She knew Jenny could not really love him and reject him after what he had gone through.

Now, she wasn't sure how to respond to him. The first topic on her mind was Jenny, as she sat next to him on her sofa. She reached for his hand and he allowed her to take his hand in hers. Then she said, "Rick, I'm going to say what I think and I hope you will not be upset with me."

He smiled and said, "I don't think you could say anything that would make be upset with you, Kathy."

She smiled and continued, "Its Jenny, Miss Jenny Brock, your lover, your future wife." She looked for his reaction and saw no expression, only a look of interest. "Rick, I cannot believe a person could truly love someone and treat them like she has treated you. Does she really love you, Rick?"

Rick had wondered about her love also when she left him in Franklin just because he wanted to find out if Middy was okay. He looked at Kathy and said, "She has made me doubt her love for me. And like I told you, she said in her note with her engagement ring that she never wanted to see me again. That's hard to take, and if she takes time to write it down, she must really mean it. Do you think so?"

Kathy could see that he had real doubt about Jenny's love. "Rick, no one can tell what someone else really thinks or feels about their love for someone. I am only telling you how it looks to me." She hesitated again and released his hand. "I will tell you something else, Rick. I don't think Jenny is right for you. You are nothing like her. You are kind, loving and compassionate with everyone. It comes natural for you. It's you. I have never seen any of these qualities in her. You deserve someone who loves and respects you for who you are."

Kathy stood up and said with a choked voice, "I'm sorry, I'm supposed to be helping you and all I'm doing is making things worse." She turned and sobbed aloud and went to the bathroom.

Rick sat and looked at his empty wine glass setting on the coffee table. He knew everything Kathy had said was right. She knew him better that Jenny did and was a much nicer person than Jenny is. Kathy was kind to everyone and gave her love to all of the employees at Vital Statistics. Why did it take this time with her to make him see what a special, loving person Kathy Crane is?

Kathy was back with red eyes and sniffing. She went directly to Rick and sat down and said, "Oh, Rick, this has been so upsetting for me and I've been so wrong trying to tell you how to live your life, please forgive me."

Rick turned to face her and said, "Kathy, first of all, there is nothing for me to forgive. You have said all of the things that have been running through my mind in the last few days. She's not anything like you and you're right, she's not like me." He placed his hand on her arm and smiled at her and then continued. "Kathy, we've known each other for over fifteen years and I consider you a very special friend, and hope you feel the same about me."

Kathy had a hard time finding her voice as she sat and looked into Rick's eyes, thinking how he was a special friend to her, but it was much more for her, she was in love with Rick and had been for a very long time. She finally cleared her throat and said, "Oh, Rick, you are very special to me."

They had been together for three hours and it was then eight o'clock. Rick knew he needed to be going, but felt so at ease with Kathy, and actually wanted to stay with her longer. He knew that was not the right thing to do. He stood up and looked down at Kathy and said, "Kathy, this has been a very special evening. I can never say enough to express how much this has meant to me. You have given me so much peace."

She stood and put her arms around him and looked up into his eyes and said, "Rick, I would never have thought we would have this special time. I've dreamed about being with you for years."

Rick wasn't sure how to respond to her comment. He

felt that he should be flattered that she wanted this special time together, but did she mean something more? He wasn't about to ask. Instead, he stood back from their embrace and held her hands in his and said, "Well, tomorrow is another workday. Thanks again and I'll see you tomorrow."

Rick walked out the door and Kathy stood there with tears of joy running down her face as she watched him walk down the hallway to the elevator.

CHAPTER

P atsy had a mission and her first step she thought, was to find Rick Stone's fiancée, Jenny. The trouble was she didn't know her last name. As most people do, she decided to use the Web, The good ole internet. She checked wedding announcements in Topeka and found her complete name. It read, Mr. Rick Stone and Jenny Brock have announced their engagement and future wedding, with the wedding date to be announced at a later date. She then checked for the address and phone number for Miss Jenny Brock and found both.

Now, her challenge was going to be how to get her to agree to meet with her. She knew she would most likely refuse to see her if she knew she was Middy's manager. She didn't want or like to lie or deceive anyone, but she had to use something to get to her.

Jenny seldom used her landline, and it rang a few times a week. Those calls were usually marketing calls. She happened to be near the phone when it rang and looked at it for a few seconds and finally on the fourth ring picked it up. She answered and started to hang up before listening to the caller, thinking she should have ignored it. Then she heard, "Miss Brock?"

Then again before she could hang up, she heard again, "Miss Brock, this is important. I need to talk with you about Rick Stone."

Jenny sat down and said, "Rick Stone? Who is this?"

"Well, Miss Brock, you don't know me, but I met Rick Stone in Franklin, Tennessee.

"Do you know Rick?"

"No, not really, but I did meet him and he told me some things I really need to share with you."

"I don't know why I should listen to you; I know Rick Stone better than anyone. I don't know how you got my number, but I think we need to end this call."

Patsy could not let her get away as she said, "He told me some things about you that you should hear. I know you are not talking with him, right?"

Jenny exhaled and said, "So, if I do agree to talk with you, how will this take place?"

Patsy was relieved and said, "I can meet you any place of your choice. If you would feel more comfortable, we can meet in a public place…this is important, Miss Brock."

She had Jenny's attention, but she knew she had to be careful. After all, there are some strange and weird people out there. "Okay, I assume you have a name. You haven't told me your name."

"You're right, I'm sorry. My name is Agnes Simpson." She used Agnes Barnes and Mary Adams (maiden name) names.

"Okay, Agnes Simpson, are you in Franklin, Tennessee now?"

She actually was as she said, "Yes I am."

Patsy waited for a long time and then Jenny said, "I am

thinking about meeting with you, but I need to think about it. I'm sure you won't give me your number, so would you call me tomorrow night, between six and seven?"

Patsy was so excited she hoped her voice stayed calm as she said, "I'll call you, and thanks."

The call ended. Patsy wanted to tell Middy but decided to wait.

CHAPTER 55

P atsy did call Jenny the next evening at 6:30. Jenny had agreed to meet with her the next day. They had agreed to meet in an open area and Jenny had requested that they meet in the local mall in Topeka. Jenny was surprised when Patsy told her that she would fly to Topeka the next morning.

The mall in Topeka was open until mid-night and this gave them plenty of time to talk. Patsy was hoping Jenny hadn't seen her on TV with Middy but couldn't worry about that now. She had to try her best to get her and Rick Stone back together. Hopefully this would not only help them but would give Middy peace.

They had agreed to meet in the main hallway just outside the J. C. Penny store. She spotted a small blonde lady sitting on one of the benches and walked up to her. "Are you Jenny Brock?"

Jenny stood and extended her hand and said, "I am, and you must be Agnes."

They both sat on the bench and smiled at each other. Patsy said, "You like something, maybe a soft drink?"

Jenny shook her head and said, "I'm okay, do you want something, Agnes?"

"No, I'm fine too. I want to thank you for seeing me and I hope our meeting will make your life better."

Jenny frowned. "Make my life better? You're not trying to sell me something are you?"

Patsy laughed and said, "I'm sorry, no it's nothing like that. I can imagine you thinking that after what I said. What I mean is your life with Rick."

Jenny was still frowning. "I still don't know what you could possibly could know about Rick that I don't know."

"Well, that's why I wanted to meet with you, to tell you how much you mean to Rick and how much he loves you." She could see that Jenny was changing her expression. She looked softer and almost smiling.

"Okay, Agnes. I'm here to listen."

Patsy had her attention now and knew she had to give it her best. "Jenny, I met Rick just after he was leaving the Vanderbilt Medical Center and had the opportunity to talk with him for quite a while. I know you knew why he was there and I also know that you were not happy with him." She continued to watch as Jenny nodded and looked more relaxed. Then she continued. "I have never seen anyone so distraught. His spirit was broken and he had been treated like a common criminal. But, the most important subject was how he kept talking about you."

"You met him outside the Vanderbilt hospital? Why was he there?"

"I thought you knew why. That is part of my reason to talk with you Jenny. He had been inside to make sure that Middy Adams, the country singer was alive and okay." Jenny's expression changed drastically. Patsy tried to ignore her expression and then continued. "You know what had happened and how Rick had been accused of harming Miss Adams. He was so relieved to learn about her being okay. He told me that he had lost the love of his life because of his visit to Middy Adam's house. Jenny, he is a broken man and his life will never be the same without you and your love. I can only imagine someone with the love he has for you. I would give anything to know that someone loved me half as much as he loves you. He needs your understanding and your love. After listening to him, I knew I had to make it my mission to tell you how much he loves you and needs you."

Jenny finally cried and hugged Patsy and said, "Oh, Agnes, without you telling me this I don't think I would have forgiven him and take him back in my life. I do love him. Oh, thank you so much."

Patsy was so relieved. They both stood and hugged once more. Jenny looked down then back to meet Patsy's eyes and said, "Will I see you again?"

Patsy looked away and then back and said, "No, I've done what I came to do. I wish you much happiness and hope you and Mr. Rick Stone have a great life."

Patsy walked away and Jenny sat on the bench and thought about Rick and the possibility of them getting back together. She needed some time to think but knew she would call him soon.

CHAPTER

R ick and Kathy had a very unusual day at the office.
Rick was almost back to his old self and had gone
out and chatted with the employees and handled calls
and emails as he always had in the past. A few wished
him good luck on his upcoming wedding. He just smiled
at the comments and made no comment to them. They
just thought he was thanking them. He had avoided much
contact with Kathy without looking like he was ignoring
her. He felt so different and knew she had to feel differently
also. She finally had to discuss some upcoming meetings
with him and check his schedule before confirming the
meetings.

She went into his office with the schedules and sat
next to him in the chair she used for dictation. His office
door was open as it usually was unless they were discussing
confidential matters. She shared the dates with him while
he checked his calendar.

After he had given her the dates, he wanted he said,
"would you close the door, please?'

Rick knew the office employees would think nothing
about the closed door, but did feel guilty, knowing what he
was about to discuss with Kathy.

She walked back to his desk and again sat in the chair next to his desk. He smiled and said, "I really slept well last night for the first time since I got back. And as I said last night, our time together has given me so much peace. You were so kind and understanding."

"Oh, Rick, this is so exciting. I slept well also, knowing our time together had helped you."

Rick became very serious and said, "I need to know what you really meant last night?"

She couldn't look at him directly as she looked down at her laced fingers and said, "You mean about how much you mean to me?"

He could tell that she was embarrassed as he said, "Kathy, please relax. I don't want to upset you. I just need to know if you meant more than just special friends."

She looked up at him then with and said, "Rick, I've never said this to you before, but I want to at this moment...I really need to say it." She wiped her tear-filled eyes with her fingers and said in a whisper, "I have loved you for so long and not just as a friend, Rick. I'm truly in love with you."

They sat in complete silence as they continued to look into each other's eyes. Finally, Rick stood and turned his back to her, and looked out the window behind his desk and said, "Kathy, I felt this was what you meant and I hope you realize this is very sudden. I know how you feel about Jenny and I know you think my relationship is over with her." He turned around to face her and said, "Well, I think it's over also, but again, this is way too sudden, too soon."

Kathy was devastated. Her face was red and her eyes were glaring at Rick. "Rick, it appears that I've made a complete fool of myself. I told you how I feel and that I am truly in love with you." She stood and continued to stare at him. "True love can never survive one sided and this love story will never happen without your love. I'm sorry to have put you in this position, I was wrong. Now, I have a lot of work to do, May I go now?"

Rick only nodded and she walked out the door and closed it behind her. He was glad she had closed the door as he needed some private time to regain his composure. He thought about the few dates he and Kathy had during their early years with Vital Statistics, but they were both young and he never felt any more than a friend, an employee with the same company and same interest. He had always like Kathy and admired her for her knowledge and desire to grow with the agency. He had asked for her to be his secretary when he was promoted to his current position and they had worked well together. Now, he knew he had upset her, but he could not let her think he was in love with her, because he wasn't and hoped they could continue to work together after this issue.

Kathy had gone directly to the lady's restroom and locked the door. She stared at herself in the mirror and said, "What is wrong with me? How could I be so stupid?" Rick had married his first wife and she was sure he had never given her a second thought and then after his divorce was engaged to Jenny Brock. Kathy realized that she had never been in the picture. Just because Jenny had treated him so badly didn't mean he would finally fall in love with her. She used the bathroom and then touched up her makeup and went back to her desk.

Rick left for lunch at noon and made no comment to Kathy as he walked by her desk. She watched him as he left the office with a feeling she had never had before, almost like someone in her life was sick or dying. She had no appetite and worked through her lunch hour. She planned to leave an hour early if Rick had no objection.

It was 3:00 when Rick returned from lunch and again, he walked by her desk without a word.

She waited until 3:45 to approach Rick. He looked up as she walked in and stood in front of his deck and said, "I need to leave an hour early today, I didn't take my lunch hour. Is it okay? Is that okay Mr. Stone?"

He had never seen her being so formal and distant with him. He was her boss, but this was ridiculous. They had always been very informal. His smile was back as he said, "Sure, Kathy, you never have to get my approval, you know that."

"Then, I'll see you tomorrow." She walked out of his office and got her purse from her desk and left the building.

Rick left just a few minutes after five and could not keep from thinking about Kathy while driving home. He had only been in his house for a few minutes when his cell rang. He first thought about Kathy but was totally shocked when he saw Jenny's name on the display. He stood frozen and could not believe she would be calling him. He let the call go to voicemail and very soon, it indicated a new voicemail. He opened the voicemail and sat at his kitchen table.

He listened as he heard a slow whine and then a whimper. "Rick, baby, I've been awful to you. I have said some things and written some things that I should have never said or written. I was upset about Middy Adams and really acted like a child. I just let it get the best of me. I love you more that life itself and I need you. I know you don't want to talk with me, but I hope you will at least listen to this message. I'm sorry, so sorry, please believe me, honey." She paused and again cried, whimpered and sniffed. Then she continued. "I love you, Rick. I don't think I can live without you. I have never wanted to take my own life, but without you and your love, I've thought about it. I need you to keep me from doing something awful." That was the end of the voicemail.

Rick closed his phone and covered his face with both hands. He could not believe what she had said. He was sure he could never truly love Jenny and knew he could never live with someone so self-centered and jealous.

His phone rang again and he was sure she must be calling back, but to his surprise, he saw Kathy's name on the display. He thought of letting it go to voicemail also but decided to answer.

"Kathy, is that you?"

There was silence on the phone and then Kathy said, "Rick, I'm sorry to bother you at home, but I feel so bad and so embarrassed. I am afraid you will never want me to work for you." She sobbed and then became silent.

Rick was very emotional himself and had to clear his throat before he could speak. He wasn't sure what to say, but he knew he needed to talk with Kathy and not on the phone. "Kathy, first of all, I could never think of working without you by my side." He hesitated and then said, "We need to talk in private and I hope you will agree."

Her voice was very soft as she said, "What do you mean in private, Rick."

"Well as you know, I offered to order pizza for us last

night, so if you will agree, I'd like to pick up one and bring it to your apartment."

"You mean now, tonight?"

She sounded better and her voice was almost back to normal. Rick smiled and said, "Yeah, like now. I do know where you live and I really want to see you so we can talk. What do you say? Do you like pepperoni, or something else?"

She softly sobbed and said, "Whatever you like will be fine with me."

"Then, it's okay for me to come over?"

"I'll be waiting."

Rick was happy and quickly changed into some jeans and a golf shirt and left for Pizza Hut.

Kathy was waiting when Rick rung her doorbell. She opened the door and smiled as he held a pizza in one hand and a six pack of Bud Light in the other. She looked at both items and said, "Well, you must be the Pizza Hut delivery man."

He smiled and said, "Yes, ma'am and I took the liberty of picking up some beers."

She stood back, waving him into her apartment for the second night in a row.

Kathy was very quiet as she took the pizza from Rick and walked to the kitchen. She set it on the kitchen table and then said, "Is pizza enough for dinner?"

Rick wanted to lighten her mood as he chuckled and said, "No, I want beer too."

She took two beers from the carton and put the other four in the fridge. She placed two paper plates on the table and opened both beers and sat down, saying nothing else.

Rick knew she was upset with him and this was the main reason he wanted to talk with her and have private time. She had been so kind and understanding with him the night before and he hoped he could help her and assure her that their friendship would not change.

They ate in silence and both seemed to enjoy the pizza and beer. Kathy broke the silence and said, "Rick, I really appreciate you coming here tonight and want us to keep the relationship we have had over the years."

Rick took his last bite and took a long swig from his beer and said, "Kathy, that's exactly why I wanted to have this time with you. I know today was very uncomfortable for both of us."

Kathy looked down at her empty paper plate and then back to meet Rick's eyes and said, "You mean uncomfortable for me, me and my run-away mouth."

Rick wanted to help her, but most of all, convince her that nothing could change his feelings and respect for her. "Kathy, I know you said some things that you may wish you had not said today."

He didn't have to wait for her response as she stood up and glared at him like she had today in his office and said, "Rick Stone, first of all, I said exactly what I feel for you. I told you that I was wrong and that I was sorry to upset you with my comments, but I do love you and am not sure I can never stop loving you." She turned and walked to her bedroom and slammed the door.

Rick sat and looked at the closed door and thought how much he really cared for Kathy but had never thought about love. He did love her, like most people did that knew her. He closed his eyes and thought about his life and his future.

He wanted to spend the rest of his life with someone who he really loved and respected and someone who felt the same way about him. Then, he thought, Kathy must feel that way about me from what she had said. Could she be that person? It seemed that the ball was in his court, so to speak. Could he fall in love with her? Was he in love with her and didn't realize that he was? So many questions and with everything he had been through in the last week, he was very confused. He sat with his eyes closed and said a silent prayer, asking God to help him make the right decision. Just as he opened his eyes and looked up, Kathy was back and standing in front of him.

Her voice was very soft and her look was hard to describe, no anger, no smile, but a look that was so intriguing. It was most calm and assured of what she was about to say. She then sat down and reached across the table and he allowed her to take his hand. She kept the same calm look and said, "Rick Stone, sometimes people don't know or understand what or who is best for them in life. I'm not qualified to analyze you or anyone else, but I probably know you better than anyone." She squeezed his hand and moved it from side to side and then continued. "Rick, I know that I love you and want to spend the rest of my life with you. The problem is... you don't know that you are really in love with me."

Rick was staring at her in total disbelief. He continued to allow her to hold his hand and then he said in a very soft voice, "Do you really believe that I am in love with you?"

She did smile then. "Rick no, I don't believe you are in love with me...I know you are in love with me. I saw you praying and I'm sure God will open your eyes to the love we have for each other. I know we were meant to be together.

Now, I've done all the talking and would like to give you the floor, Rick Stone. I want you to tell me that you don't love me and don't want to spend your life with me, the person who loves you more than anyone in the world."

Rick pulled his hand away from hers and placed both hands over his face. His emotions were completely out of control. He sat in silence and then cried.

She waited and remained silent, waiting for him to respond.

He slowly placed his hands on the table and looked at her with tears running down his face. "Kathy, I have thought about you forever, but truly, never as a lover, but at this moment, I do feel differently."

"You mean you feel love?"

He couldn't keep from smiling as he said, "It must be love, what else could it be?"

She stood and said, "Rick, I need to hold you but most of all I need you to hold me. I love you with all my heart and like I've said, you do love me also."

They embraced with full body contact and could not resist kissing. They had known each other for over fifteen years and had never kissed each other on the lips. They had over the years kissed each other on the cheek on special occasions, like congratulations for achievements and promotions, but Rick had never felt attracted to her sexually. That feeling had always been from Kathy.

Their kiss had been very brief and Kathy knew she should not be aggressive this early. She knew Rick loved her, but she also knew he needed time to accept the fact, and she was prepared to wait until he made the next move to confirm his love for her.

As they stood back from their embrace, both smiling, Rick said, "I have a voicemail on my phone that I would like share with you, Kathy."

Kathy frowned and said, "A voicemail?"

They went to the living room and sat on the sofa. Rick placed his phone on the coffee table and activated the voicemail with the speaker on. It was Jenny's voicemail that he had just received earlier in the evening. They both listened in total silence.

When it was over, Rick closed his phone and said, "I guess this confirms some of your feelings about Jenny."

Kathy only nodded and then looked deeply into Rick's eyes. Then she said, "Rick, we both know she is not the person you want to spend your life with."

They both knew there was nothing else to talk about and Rick soon left, thanking Kathy and said he would see her in the morning.

They both knew this evening together was going to change their lives forever.

CHAPTER

P atsy was so excited and could hardly wait to tell Middy the good news. She got back to the house after midnight and Middy was already asleep. She went to her bedroom downstairs and tried to sleep but couldn't. She knew Middy wouldn't mind be awaken with the great news she had. As she was getting up and starting upstairs, she heard Middy outside her door. She opened the door and Middy stood there smiling.

"Well, do you have good news? I waited up until eleven and then got sleepy and went to bed. I must have heard you come in and just now woke up."

Patsy went to her and put her arms around her and said, "Oh, Middy, it went so well. Jenny Brock is going to forgive Rick and take him back. I've been so excited; I started to call you from Topeka, but really wanted to tell you in person."

Middy smiled and said, "You're sure? Did she say she would get back with Rick?"

"Yes, Middy, I have no doubt. She cried and said she just let herself get carried away about Rick being with you. She is very jealous, I'm sure you know that."

She kissed Patsy on the cheek and said, "Well, that's one problem I can put to rest, thanks to you." She left and went back upstairs.

Patsy went to bed and hoped Middy would put this out of her mind now. She knew Middy had other issues in her life that still bothered her. She was afraid she would always worry about Beth, her half-sister, but most of all, if she could be pregnant. Her singing career was still doubtful in Middy's mind, but Patsy felt she would be okay with her future as a singer if she could get these other issues settled.

Patsy slept and dreamed about Agnes Barnes.

CHAPTER

Kathy was in the office the next morning at her normal time, at 7:00 and was feeling very excited about her future... her future with Rick Stone.

Rick's phone rang just before nine, and Kathy answered as usual with, "Rick Stone's office, this Kathy. She almost dropped her phone as she heard the caller say, "Kathy, this is Jenny Brock. May I speak to Rick, please?"

Kathy's heart was pounding as she sat stunned, and unable to fine her voice.

"Kathy, are you there?"

She was there but wanted to be somewhere else at that moment. She cleared her throat and said, "Yes, I'm here. Sorry, Jenny, he's late, uh, I mean he won't be until later."

She could hear Jenny exhale and say, "Do you know if his cell phone is working?"

Kathy knew her expression revealed her shock and hoped no one in the office noticed. Again, she hesitated long enough for Jenny to ask again, "Are you there, Kathy? Is something wrong? You sound different, is Rick okay?"

Kathy finally calmed herself and said, "Jenny, everything's okay, I'm just a little under the weather this morning. And to answer your question, I don't know if Rick's cell phone is working, I seldom call it."

There was more silence on the phone and then Jenny said, "Well I did get his voicemail last night and left a message, but he hasn't returned my call. Please ask him to call me when he gets in." She paused again and said, "And Kathy, I hope you get to feeling better." The line went dead.

Kathy got up and went to the lady's room and locked the door. She needed the privacy to hopefully prepare for what was to come when Rick arrived later in the morning.

When Rick arrived, most of the office staff had gone to lunch. He was all smiles and looked happy and refreshed. Kathy smiled and hoped what she had to tell Rick would not spoil his day...their day."

He walked to her desk and said, "How are you today, Kathy?"

She felt sick to her stomach but continued to give him her best smile. "Well, I've been better."

"Oh, are you okay? You look a little pale."

She then said, "I need to see you in your office, Rick."

She followed him in and closed the door. He could not remember seeing her looking so distraught and worried.

"Kathy, you're not looking well, are you sure you're okay?"

Kathy followed Rick into his office, closing the door and then sat down in one of the chairs across from Rick's desk and said, "It's Jenny.

"Jenny? You're worried about Jenny? I thought we had settled that last night. Please don't worry about her."

Kathy closed her eyes and said, "She called this morning."

Rick raised his eyebrows and said, "Well, I guess I shouldn't be surprised after her voicemail last night. What did she say?"

"Well, she asked for you and I told her you would be in later and she wants you to call her." She hesitated and then said, "She told me about leaving you a voicemail and asked if your cell was working."

They both sat in silence for a long time, and then Kathy said, "Rick, I know what you said last night, but I'm so worried about you talking with her. If she convinces you to take her back…" Tears filled her eyes. She couldn't continue.

Rick wanted to hold her and tell her that he loved her but could not do that in his office. He finally said, "Kathy, I've thought about our conversation last night and know you are right. I am convinced we were meant to be together and I not only think I'm in love with you." He smiled and said in a choked voice, "I am in love with you and want you to believe me."

Kathy was visibly shaken as she said in an almost whisper, "Oh, Rick I do believe you. I just want this to be over and our lives to continue. I love you so much."

He looked at her for a long moment and said, "I'm going to do something that will hopefully convince you once and for all of my love for you Kathy."

She looked shocked and said, "Do something? What are you saying?"

He smiled and said, "I want you to sit right there and listen to me when I talk with Jenny."

Kathy didn't want to cry again but could not control herself. Between sobs she said, "Oh, Rick, I don't know what to say. You are so sweet and loving."

He reached for his phone and said, "Don't' say anything…just listen."

He then called Jenny's cell number.

CHAPTER

Kathy was surprised that Rick would let her listen to his conversation with Jenny and could not believe it when he put the phone on speaker.

It was obvious that Jenny had Rick's number on her cell as she answered. "Oh, Rick." She paused and then cried aloud for a long time. Rick and Kathy sat and listened to her sobs.

Rick finally interrupted her crying and said, "Jenny, you wanted me to call you."

"Oh, yes and thank you for calling be back. Rick, I don't know where to begin. I've been a fool, an awful person. I know the things I've said to you and the terrible note I left on your front porch have been devastating to you. I want to tell you how much I love you and ask for your forgiveness. I just let my jealousy cloud my mind. I know you love me and I also know you were just a victim in the Middy Adams situation." She paused again and cried for a long time.

Rick again spoke over her sobs. "Jenny, first of all, I really have nothing to say to you. You have hurt me more than anyone ever has in my entire life. If you had really loved me, you could never have said and done the things you did." He paused and looked at Kathy and then continued.

"I want and need someone I can love and know their love for me is real, real enough to understand and not jump to conclusions as you did with me. My heart was broken when you left me in Franklin, Tennessee, and even more so when I read your note and found your engagement ring with our wedding announcement. So, Jenny, I have nothing more to say to you. I do hope you find someone in the future and I also hope you will treat them with respect and real love, the kind of love people expect from the person they want to spend their life with."

He started to push the disconnect button on his phone when she said, "Wait!"

He paused and frowned at the phone as she said, "I've sat here and listened to how bad you think I've been to you and I have also tried to tell you how sorry I am for what happened between us. From what you are saying, you won't even try to make this work for us. I just need to hear you say that."

"Jenny, I thought I had said that, but if you want me to confirm it, you are exactly right. Our lives are over. Please do not try to contact me in the future."

Before he could disconnect, they heard her say, "I hope you and Middy Adams rot in hell. I hate you, Rick Stone." She was still talking as Rick closed his phone.

Rick looked at Kathy and shook his head and said, "Well, I'm sure glad to know her true feelings." He hesitated and then said, "Kathy, I really think we are both blessed to be together and know what real love and respect means."

Kathy could not think of anything to add as she sat and looked into his eyes and smiled. She knew their love was real and was happier than she had ever been in her life.

CHAPTER

Patsy felt that she needed to let Jenny Brock know who she was and hopefully wouldn't be angry with her. After all, she had been the one to get her and Rick Stone back together. She again called her home number later in the afternoon and the phone rang several times and as she was about to hang up, she heard a very weak voice.

She wasn't sure if she had called the correct number and asked, "Is this Jenny Brock's residence?"

Her voice was hoarse and weak. "Yes, this is Jenny Brock. How did you get my number?"

Patsy smiled and said, "Oh, Jenny this is Agnes Simpson. I just wanted to call you and make sure you were able to get back with Rick Stone."

There was complete silence on the phone and Patsy said, "Jenny, you still there?"

"Yes, I'm here, Agnes, but not in very good spirits."

"Oh, I'm sorry, Jenny. I hope you are not sick. I just was hoping you and Rick had gotten back together. He was so anxious to have you back. I'm not trying to butt into your private life."

"I'm sure you're not, Agnes, but somehow, your information was all wrong about Rick wanting me."

"All wrong? I don't understand. After what he told me I'm sure he wants you back. Have you actually talked with him?"

Jenny's voice was cracking as she said, "Oh, yes and I'm sure he wants to be with that Middy Adams. I did talk with him this morning in fact and he told me to never try to contact him again. I know you wanted to help, but it's over for Rick and me."

Patsy was totally shocked. She was so sure Rick would welcome Jenny back with open arms. What could have possibly gone wrong? She had called to be sure they were back together, but most of all, she wanted to tell Jenny who she was and tell her that she was Patsy Holt. She was so glad she hadn't told her in the beginning of their conversation. She knew she could never let her know that Middy Adams' manager had been the one who tried to get them back together. She couldn't think of anything to say except how sorry she was that it hadn't worked. "Jenny, I'm sorry to have bothered you and especially sorry things have not worked out with you and Rick."

Jenny sobbed and said, "It's okay, it's not your fault. I made all of this happen and will have to live with it. Goodbye, Agnes."

Patsy started to say goodbye, but the phone went dead.

Patsy sat and stared at the TV in her bedroom and thought how happy Middy had been, knowing that Rick and Jenny were back together. This would still be one of the issues Middy would feel guilty about. Then, she thought, how would Middy know? Do I have to tell her?

CHAPTER

Rick and Kathy had a busy afternoon and had not spoken about Jenny since the phone call at noon. They both worked until a little after six. By the time Rick came out of his office, all of the staff had gone and Kathy was alone at her desk, finishing up her reports for the day.

Rick stopped at her desk and said, "Well, it looks like you and I will have to close up."

Kathy looked up from her work and said, "I'm just about finished, maybe another minute."

"It's okay, I'll wait."

She closed her desk and locked it. "I have closed before, lots of times when you were not here, Mr. Stone."

"I know you have, Miss Crane, but I want to leave with you and take you to dinner."

She stood and looked around the darkened general office and then kissed him. He held her in his arms and said, "So, does that mean you will go to dinner with me."

She laughed and said, "Who needs to use words when your lips can answer for you?"

He laughed also and said, "Maybe if we could go to your apartment tonight you could use your lips to talk with. What do you think?"

She kissed him again and then said, "That one says, YES in case you don't understand lip language yet."

She followed him to his house and waited in her car. He was out within five minutes carrying an overnight bag and a clothing bag over his shoulder. She smiled as she thought about spending the night with him, hopefully in her bed.

After a nice dinner at one of the best restaurants in Topeka, he followed her to her apartment. They spent a long time learning to talk using lip language and did end up in Kathy's king size bed.

Kathy was up the next morning, before Rick and had coffee and breakfast started when he wandered in to the kitchen. "Boy that smells so good."

She went to him and kissed him and said, "Are you talking about me, or the breakfast?"

He laughed and said, "That's one of those loaded questions. I think I'll be safe saying, you and the breakfast."

"Good answer, how do you like your eggs?"

They both knew they had found the right person and couldn't be happier. They also knew they had to think about their future, but for now, they were just going enjoy every moment they could be together.

CHAPTER

atsy and Middy had never kept anything from each other. This was one time that Patsy wanted to keep what she had learned from Jenny Brock to herself, but knew she had to tell her. She was waiting for the best time and thought that later in the morning, after breakfast, would be the time to tell her.

They had eaten breakfast together from the very beginning of their partnership. It was a happy time of the day, and most times it was very late morning and many times in early afternoon.

Middy seemed more happy than usual on that morning. She sipped her coffee and smiled at Patsy and said, "Honey, when I am sad or down about anything, you have always been there for me to bring me back." Her smile, however, was not typical, Patsy knew her better than anyone, and could see the concern in her pretty blue eyes.

Patsy knew she couldn't eat anything. It was difficult enough to drink her coffee. Her stomach was in a knot, knowing what she had to tell Middy.

Middy had noticed how Patsy seemed quiet and said, "Well, you seem quiet this morning. Did your trip to Topeka wear you out? I know it was a quick turnaround for you."

Patsy knew waiting would only make it worse as she said, "Middy, I have some news about Rick that I hate to have to tell you."

Middy glared at Patsy and said, "Patsy, don't tell me that something has happened to Rick Stone." She continued glaring at Patsy, waiting for her answer.

"Middy, I told you about Jenny and was sure that Rick would welcome her with open arms.

"And?"

"And, he didn't, Middy."

"And just how do you know?"

"I talked with Jenny last evening and she told me. She told me that Rick said he never wanted to see her again. I'm sorry Middy."

Middy covered her face with both hands and said, "Is God trying to punish me? Oh, Patsy, I was so happy hearing that Jenny was going to take Rick back. What could have happened?"

"She didn't say but did say it was her fault for the way she had treated Rick. Who knows, in time they might work out things. You have enough to worry about without thinking about Rick and Jenny. So, please try to put this out of your mind. We've done all we can and you should not feel guilty."

Middy looked up and shook her head. "Oh, Patsy I don't know if I can handle any more."

Patsy went around the table and put her hand on her shoulder. "Honey, there won't be any more. Now, let's try to think positive. There won't be anything else."

Middy stood and looked into Patsy's eyes and said, "I'm

a week late with my period. I'm so afraid that I'm pregnant. It looks like there will be something else."

Patsy couldn't speak. She held Middy and they both cried. She knew now that had been the reason for Middy's look of concern.

CHAPTER

Rick Stone was usually the last person to leave the office and this day was no different. Kathy would always check with him before she left to ask if he needed anything. He looked up and saw her standing there with a smile on her face

He smiled and said, "Are you leaving now?"

"Yes, but as always, Mr. Rick Stone, do you need anything before I leave?"

He laughed and said, "Well, Miss Crane, I'm good for now, but I will need something when I get to your apartment."

"Oh, you're going to my apartment. I can't imagine what you could need there, but I'm sure you can show me when you get there." She winked at him and walked out of his office.

Kathy had changed into a pair of shorts and a tank top and was waiting for Rick to arrive. She jumped up as she heard the doorbell. She opened the door and said, "Oh, so you did come to see me, Mr. Stone."

He took her in his arms and kissed her after closing the door. They stood back from each other and locked eyes. Rick finally said, "Kathy, I only hope we can continue our love for the rest of our lives. I love you more than I can put into words." He kissed her again and continued. "And please never lose your sense of humor."

She knew they loved having fun and kidding each other as she continued to smile at him.

Rick went to the bathroom and then to the bedroom to change into shorts and a t shirt. He came into the den and saw that Kathy had two wine glasses filled for them, setting on the coffee table. He sat next to her and said, "Thanks for the wine." He took a sip and then said, "I've got something to discuss with you, Kathy."

"As usual, I'm all ears, what are we going to discuss?"

He set his wine down and said, "I want to talk about Middy Adams."

She frowned and said, "You want to talk about Middy Adams?"

Rick put his hand on her knee and said, "I know you are surprised by my comment, but this is about us."

"About us... What do you mean about us?"

"Yes, it is about us, Kathy. Just think about it for a moment. Before I went to Tennessee with Middy, I was engaged to Jenny." He smiled and looked deeply into her eyes. "Now, because of my involvement with Middy Adams, I have found my true love."

Kathy kissed him and said, Oh, Rick, that's true and I could not be happier, but I thought we had already talked about Middy and her involvement in our lives. So, what else can we discuss about her. I really don't understand."

"Well, yes, we have discussed her and my involvement with her, but I want us to talk with her."

"You want *us* to talk with Middy Adams, why?"

Rick knew she did not understand and he was not explaining what he wanted to do. "Kathy, Middy left me a voice mail the day I got home from Tennessee and wanted to tell me how sorry she was and causing me to lose my bride-to-be. She asked me to call her back and I did not call her. I feel bad that I didn't call her back. I know she must be upset with me. Kathy, as I said, I want us to go and talk with her. I really need to get this behind me and have us go on with our lives. I am also hopeful that talking with her will give her peace and she can also put this behind her."

Kathy cleared her throat and said, "So, you can just call her and ask for a meeting with her?"

Rick smiled and said, "Yes, in fact, she gave me her personal cell number and asked me to call her. I'm sure she will agree to see us. I hope you understand my need to do this, Kathy."

She kissed him again and said, "I do understand and would be disappointed if you did not want to get this behind us."

Middy was surprised to see Rick Stone's name appear on the display of her cell phone. She remembered giving him her private number, but never thought he would actually call her. She had just talked with Patsy about the possibility of being pregnant and now looking at her phone and hearing it ring, only added to her distress. She let it go to voicemail and looked across the table at Patsy.

Patsy could see the concern on her face and said, "What is it, one of those crazy calls?"

"It's Rick Stone."

Patsy stood up and said, "I'll call him and stop this, Middy. You don't need any more distress. I can't imagine why he would call you; knowing he did not return your call when you wanted to tell him how sorry you were. I'll let him know how we both feel about him.

Middy hesitated and then said, "Use my phone." She handed her phone to Patsy.

Patsy took the phone and said, "Do you want to listen?"

Middy closed her eyes and only nodded.

Back in Topeka, Rick had listened to Middy's voicemail, which was simple. The voicemail only said, "This person is not available to take your call." He looked at Kathy and said, "I'm sure she'll call me."

The call did come and it was only a few minutes later. Rick smiled when his phone rang and he saw Middy's name on his display. He looked at Kathy as he answered with, "Middy is this you?"

There was silence for a moment and then he heard Patsy Holt say, "No, Rick, it's Patsy Holt."

Rick was still smiling at Kathy as he said, "Oh, Patsy, how are you?"

More silence and then Patsy said, "This is not about me, Rick. I'm calling you to ask you, or I should say tell you not to call Middy." She paused again and then continued. "First of all, I cannot believe you would call Middy after the way you treated her when she tried to apologize to you and never called her back. All she wanted was to tell you how sorry she was, so no Mr. Rick Stone she don't want to talk with you."

Rick was at a loss for words. His phone was on speaker and Kathy was frowning and staring at the phone. He finally cleared his throat and said in a very soft voice, "Patsy, that's the reason I'm calling, I have been ashamed of my behavior and want to tell Middy how sorry I am for not calling her back."

More silence and then Patsy said, "Well, it's a little late for that, but I'll tell her why you finally called."

"Patsy, I want to tell her myself, please let me speak to her."

After a long pause Patsy said, "No." The phone went dead.

Rick and Kathy sat and stared at the phone. Kathy finally said, "Rick, you tried and that's all you can do."

Rick looked at her and said, "I still need to tell her."

Kathy knew how strongly Rick felt about talking with Middy and wished she could do something to help him put this behind him. Just as she was having this thought Rick's cell rang.

His phone was still lying on the coffee table and they both stared at the display, showing Middy's name.

Rick looked at Kathy and said, "Patsy must have forgotten something else she wanted to make sure that I understood." He pushed the talk button and said, "Okay, Patsy, what else do you want to say?"

There was silence for a few seconds and then Rick and Kathy looked at each other in total shock as they heard a soft sweet voice. "Rick, its Middy." The speaker was on.

Rick was shocked to hear Middy's voice since Patsy Hold had made it clear that Middy was not going to talk with him. He looked at Kathy and then said, "Middy, I'm so happy to hear your voice. I hope all is well with you and I am so pleased that you called me."

Middy was speaking very softly and slowly as she said, "Rick, you know how bad I feel about your treatment while you were here in Tennessee and most of all, the breakup that I caused with you and Jenny. I understand how upset you have been with me and now, finally I can tell you how sorry I am and ask for your forgiveness." She then sobbed softly.

Rick waited for her to regain her composure and then said, "Middy, I need to tell you something, first of all I do forgive you and know you had nothing to do with what happened to me. It's true, I was very upset with you when you called me, but because of your involvement, my life is wonderful now."

"Your life is wonderful because of my involvement? Rick, I have no idea what you are saying."

Rick could not keep from looking at Kathy and smiling before he said, "Middy, I know this sounds crazy, but Jenny Brock and I are no longer engaged, in fact, we are never going to see each other again."

"And I made that happen, I made you lose your true love, it breaks my heart, Rick."

"Middy, I need you to believe me, I am happier than I have ever been. Jenny was not meant to be my wife. If she had loved me like she said she did, she would have helped me when I needed her the most. Middy, she never loved me and I'm so thankful that I found out before we married."

"Rick, this is all so strange to me. I want to believe you, but most of all I really want you to be okay and have a happy life."

"Middy, I have a request and hope you will grant my request." He paused, looked at Kathy again and said, "I want to meet with you and bring my true love with me so she can meet you also."

"You mean come here and help me understand what you are telling me now? You would bring your true love?"

"Middy, as I said, I know this all sounds crazy, but I know if we can all three sat down together, you will understand and hopefully give you peace once and for all."

"Rick, I need to have the peace you are talking about and your forgiveness most of all. I will wait till we can meet and it sounds like you will bring a special person with you. Rick, now I want to see you, but I have one condition."

"Condition?"

"Yes, it's a long way from Topeka, Kansas to Franklin, Tennessee and I will have a private jet pick you up and bring you and your special person here. Now, before you speak, that is my condition. All I need to know is when do you want to come, I'm available now and will be for a while longer."

Rick looked into Kathy's eyes and then said, "We could come tomorrow, or the next day."

"Then tomorrow is okay?"

It was obvious that Middy wanted this meeting as soon as possible. Rick was also ready to get this over and explain how Middy had actually changed his life and hopefully give both of them the peace they so badly needed. It was agreed that Rick and Kathy would travel to Nashville the next day.

CHAPTER

R ick smiled as the pilot came into the waiting area at the
Topeka private terminal. He was the same pilot that he
and Middy had flown to Nashville with. They shook
hands and Rick introduced him to Kathy. They were soon
on the private jet with seat belts secured and taking off,
headed to Nashville.

Kathy had never been on a private jet and was very
impressed with the plane and the friendly pilot and co-pilot.
The flight was very smooth and they were soon making the
final approach in Nashville.

Middy had told Rick that transportation would be
provided for them at the private terminal. They walked
into the waiting area and Rick immediately recognized
Patsy Holt, standing just inside the doorway. She smiled
and walked to Rick and hugged him. Rick stood back and
said, "This is Kathy Crane."

Patsy opened her arms and gave Kathy a hug and said,
"It's a Middy Adams thing, we never shake hands, we only
hug. It's so nice to meet you, Kathy."

Kathy couldn't believe how friendly and down to earth
Patsy was with her.

"I hope your flight was pleasant and smooth, those guys

do a great job." They were soon in Patsy's car and headed south on I-65.

As they drove through the front gate, Patsy waved at the guard and then parked in the circle drive in front of the house.

As they entered the huge foyer, Kathy was impressed as most people were on their first visit. She looked at Patsy and said, "It is so beautiful, I'm sure you and Middy love living here."

Patsy thought how so many people said the same thing and how she didn't really feel that it was such a wonderful place, but they had to live somewhere like this with the security and privacy it gave them. She only smiled and said, "Yes, it is beautiful."

Their attention was then drawn to the sound of Middy's voice as she stood at the top of the stairs. "Welcome, I'm so happy to see you all."

She then walked down the stairs and went directly to Rick and took him in her arms and they hugged for a long time. She finally stood back and said, "Thanks, Rick, thanks for coming." She then turned to face Kathy and said, "This must be that very special person you told me about on the phone."

Rick put his arm around Kathy's shoulder and said, "Yes, Middy. She is the love of my life. I am happy to introduce you to Kathy Crane."

Kathy knew what was coming and took a step toward Middy as they both opened their arms and hugged.

They stood back, holding hands and Middy said, "Kathy, I'm so glad to meet you." She hesitated and looked at Rick and then said, "I don't have to tell you what a special person Rick Stone is. You are so blessed to have found him."

Kathy had tears in her eyes as she hugged Middy again and said, "Thank you; I really appreciate you saying that. I love him with all my heart."

Patsy had stood and listened to the conversation and could see that this meeting was something Middy really needed. She stepped in closer the group and said, "Well, I'm sure you two would like to have a few minutes to get settled in and get ready for dinner."

Rick and Kathy looked at each other and Rick said, "Yeah that sounds good."

Patsy pointed toward the hallway and said, "Let me show you two to your bedroom."

Rick and Kathy were surprised that Patsy seemed to accept them sharing a bedroom and smiled as they followed her to the guest bedroom.

After they entered the bedroom and closed the door behind them, Kathy said, "Rick this is so different than I would have ever expected. It's like being with a friend or a relative. They are so nice and very kind."

Rick kissed her and said, "Honey, they are both very kind and just people like us. Middy's fame and fortune has not changed her. She is the same person I met when she was looking for her father."

Kathy smiled and said, "Yeah, I remember you telling me about your first meeting with her."

Rick looked at her and thought how lucky he was to have fallen in love with her and was so happy and looking forward to her becoming his wife.

Meanwhile, Middy and Patsy were upstairs in Middy's

small kitchen sitting across from each other. Middy was looking happier than Patsy had seen her since the terrible attack. She reached for her hand and said, "Honey, I'm so happy to see you looking like your old self. I know this time with Rick will be very special for you and want it to be your special time."

Middy squeezed her hand and said, "Oh, I'm so looking forward to this time with him also." She paused and then said, "But, I don't want this to be just Rick and me. I want you, as always to be by my side and I think it would be unfair to not include his sweet Kathy.

Patsy knew she would want this arrangement but wanted her to know that she would understand if she wanted time with Rick alone.

Their maid had been there all day, preparing a dinner for their guest and they were looking forward to a great meal with Rick and Kathy.

CHAPTER

Rick and Kathy heard a soft knock on their door and Rick opened it to see Middy standing there with a beautiful smile. She opened her arms again to Rick and looked at Kathy and said, "Dinner is ready, you guys ready to eat?"

Kathy could see how Rick being there was so special for Middy. She could not imagine them not wanting some private time alone, and really expected it to happen.

Rick broke their embrace and turned to Kathy and said, "You ready, Honey?"

She nodded and then walked to Middy and they hugged also. Then, the three of them walked into the formal dining room. Patsy was waiting for them and she gave both Rick and Kathy hugs.

Middy and Patsy sat side by side, facing Rick and Kathy. The maid, Miss Charlotte came to the table and asked for drink orders. Rick and Kathy looked at each other and Middy said, "We have some of everything." She looked at Charlotte and said, "I'll get us started, Merlot wine for me."

Charlotte then looked at the guest and they both agreed with Middy's choice. Patsy chose white zinfandel. They were all enjoying the wine and having small talk about their flight and how great it was to have this opportunity.

Middy looked at Kathy and said, "So, are you all going to marry in Topeka?"

Kathy took a sip of her wine and looked at Rick and then said, "Well, to be honest, he hasn't asked me yet."

They all laughed and Middy frowned at Rick and said, "Well, Mr. Rick Stone, what are you waiting for?"

Rick smiled and then said, "Well, I'm sure she knows I want to marry her."

Middy frowned again and said, "Oh, come on, Rick, when are you are going to ask this sweet girl?"

"Okay, Miss Middy Adams, I can't think of a better place than here… tonight."

Kathy looked at Rick with her mouth open but did not speak.

Rick stood and looked down at Kathy and said, "Well, I never thought about asking you in this present company, but just think, how many people have Middy Adams as a witness?"

Kathy had tears in her eyes as she said, "Rick, witnesses or not, you know my answer before you ask."

Middy, Patsy and Rick all laughed at her comment, then Middy and Patsy stood also.

Kathy slowly stood as Rick got down on one knee and ask the obvious question. After Kathy's answer, he stood and took her in his arms and they kissed for a long time. After they stood back from each other, Middy and Patsy gave hugs to Rick and Kathy.

All four had tears in their eyes as Middy finally said, "I will always remember this special evening." She paused and looked at Kathy and said, "Thank you for sharing this special moment with us. I think it's time for a toast as she held her glass high and said, "Congratulations to a very sweet couple, may your days be filled with love and happiness."

After they had all clicked their glasses, Middy looked at Rick and frowned again with her humor and said, "I know you were not prepared for this to happen and did not have a ring with you, but I want you to have this one." She held out her hand, showing a full carat diamond ring and said, "Rick, please take this ring as my wedding gift to you two, and place it on your future wife's finger."

Rick wasn't surprised as he knew how thoughtful Middy could be. He slowly removed the ring and turned to Kathy and took her left hand and placed it on her ring finger. There was total silence in the room as everyone felt the special meaning of this moment.

Kathy finally broke the silence as she looked at Middy and said, "Middy, this is so sweet." She looked down at the ring and then said, "I can never tell you what this means to me, it's not the value of this beautiful ring, but who it came from, and knowing that it is something you wanted to do for Rick and me."

Middy smiled and said, "Thank you for your kind words."

After they had finished their dinner, Kathy looked at Rick and then back at Middy and said, "Middy, I know Rick wanted to meet with you so you two could have some private time." She then looked at Patsy and continued. "I'm sure Patsy and I can visit while you two have your time alone."

Middy smiled and said, "Kathy, you are so sweet and understanding. Rick and I do need this special time."

Middy took Rick's hand and said, "Let's go upstairs."

Kathy and Patsy both smiled at each other and knew this was a time they both needed.

Middy and Rick sat in the small kitchen, but the table was different from the one Rick remembered. He sat and put his hand on the tabletop and said, "Is this a new table?"

Middy laughed and said, "Everything is new, Patsy thought the old furnishings would bring back memories that I need to forget."

"And are you forgetting…that night?"

Middy sat down across from Rick and said, "I'm trying, really trying, but I'm sure I'll never forget that night."

Rick frowned and said, "I'm sure you're right, I just wish it had never happened. I am so sorry you had this terrible thing to happen to you."

"Rick, you also, because of me bringing you here, had an awful time and I can never forgive myself for what I caused."

Rick reached for her hand and said, "Yes, we both had a very bad time and you could have died from your injuries. In my case, it was very traumatic, but because of what happened, I found my true love. I just hope you are able to put this behind you and go on with your life, your career. Your fans are looking for Middy Adams to reappear so they can hear that beautiful voice and see your pretty face and sweet smile.

Middy looked very serious as she said, "Well, I appreciate your concern for me and my future." She paused and then said, "I need some more wine. Would you have another glass with me?"

Rick smiled and nodded but wondered what could be so serious.

Middy brought two glasses of merlot and sat one in front of Rick. She sat down and took a sip and then said, "I've been drinking more that I should lately, but that will stop soon."

"Well, that's good, Middy. It's understandable with the stress you've had, I'm glad you are going to slow down and drink less."

"Not less Rick. You see, I have to quit totally for at least the next nine months."

"Nine months?" Rick voice was a whisper. Then he wondered if she thought he had had sex with her...raped her.

She could see the concern on his face. She took another drink and said, "Yes Rick, I've missed my period and am sure I must be pregnant, but you're not involved. I had a rape test, including DNA and know the identity."

"The guy who attacked you?"

"Yes, and he also attacked you. His name was Jimmy Skaggs."

"Was?"

"Yes, he was arrested and charged with rape and attempted murder. Before he was scheduled for trial, he hanged himself in his jail cell."

Rick put his hands on his face and closed his eyes. Here was Middy Adams sharing her deepest and private life with him. He knew they had a good relationship, but with her sharing this with him was very special. He was sure no one besides Patsy Holt had heard her talk about this like she had with him.

Middy knew her comments were shocking to Rick, to

say the least. She sat and waited for him to look at her as he was still sitting with his face covered with both hands.

He finally did look at Middy with tears in his eyes and said, "Middy, I am so touched that you would tell me all of this about your life, it means so much to me to know you feel that at ease with me."

Middy smiled and said, "Rick, I've liked you since our first meeting when I was trying to find my father. You seemed so kind and really interested in helping me." She paused and laughed softly and said, "And yes, I do remember you asking me to have dinner with you."

Rick was shaking his head and smiling. "Yes, I really wanted to see you again, but you were totally focused on finding your father, and I remembered you saying you were too busy to date."

They both sat in silence and continued to smile at each other.

"Middy, I do have a question about our relationship."

"Our relationship?" Middy said with raised eyebrows.

"I have wondered about your call to me and then bringing me here, in fact, to this very room." He waited for her to respond.

Middy took another drink of wine and seemed to be embarrassed. She tilted her head and said, "Rick, I was lonely and scared. Patsy had left me and I needed her more than I realized. She and I had been together since my career started. I'm not an independent person; I need someone in my life, someone to give me support and love. I was sure she would never come back and like I said, I needed someone. I remembered how kind you had been to me and thought you could be that person to give me the support and yes, love that I need in my life."

Rick was sure he knew the answer to his next question, but wanted it confirmed by Middy. "So, you really wanted me as a manager and a support person, like you said, not as a lover, right?"

Middy did not hesitate as she said, "Rick, I do love you, but not like a lover, or a husband. Patsy and I have a special relationship that no one can understand. We're not lovers, like some think. It's true that Patsy is gay and it is the reason she left me. She found a lover and thought she had found her lifetime love, just like you feel about Kathy, but that did not work out and she is back with me and committed her life to me. Rick, I know I mislead you and if we had not been attacked that night, we may have had a sexual relationship." She paused and then said, "Rick, like we both have said, this has all worked out for both of us. I am going to make it through this and you have found the love of your life. We both have so much to be thankful for."

Rick stood and walked around the table and Middy stood, facing him. They hugged for a long time and then broke their embrace. As they walked down the stairs, they both knew this private time had been a turning point in their lives. They both felt the relief they needed and were ready to go forward with their futures. Rick was happier than he had ever been. He knew everything that had happened between him and Middy had allowed him to find the love of his life. He truly hoped that Middy would now be able to go on with her life and most of all, not be pregnant from this violent attack.

Middy also was grateful for the peace she now had with

Rick, but still had the pregnancy possibility hanging over her head and the guilt feeling she had about her involvement with William Hatcher and the things she had said to him. Now, that he was dead she would never have the opportunity to ask for his forgiveness. She still was not at peace about him and wondered if she ever would be.

CHAPTER

T he next morning, Rick and Kathy had a light breakfast with Middy and Patsy and then Patsy took the love birds to the airport. They went to the private terminal and again met the same pilot and co-pilot, waiting for them in the small waiting area. They were soon boarded and Patsy watched from the window as they took off, heading back to Topeka and a happy life together. Patsy smiled and thought how all of this had finally worked out for everyone. Then, she thought about Middy and knew she still had issues keeping her from returning to her life that she and Middy had enjoyed until she had decided to leave her for Agnes.

She wanted to do everything possible to help Middy and as she drove from the airport, she thought of one thing that could help her. Before getting back on I-65, she stopped at a drug store and went to the pharmacy and bought a pregnancy test and asked the pharmacist how accurate the test was. He told her that they had been very accurate, but to contact a doctor should they have any doubt. Patsy thanked him and then drove back to Franklin and hoped she could convince Middy to use it.

Middy was on her phone when she walked into the

house, sitting in the downstairs dining room. She covered the phone with her hand and said, "Its Mom and Dad."

Patsy smiled and said, "Tell them hello."

She then went to her bathroom and opened the instructions that came with the pregnancy test, and again, hoped that Middy would agree to use it.

Middy had talked with her parents more than usual since she had returned from the hospital. The conversations were comforting for Middy and her parents. She ended her call and then called out for Patsy.

Patsy had just come out from the bathroom and said, "Hey, I'm here," as she walked into the dining room and then said, "Your mom and dad doing okay?"

"Yeah, they are really doing fine, and said they sent their love to you."

Patsy again felt that lump in her stomach, knowing they had no idea about her not being with Middy. She knew she had to tell them as soon as she got Middy back to normal and, was going to try to work on that now.

Patsy had the instructions from the pregnancy test in her hand as she said, "I bought something for you."

Middy laughed and then said, "What, something for me and it's not even my birthday."

Patsy sat next to her at the table and said, "This… is the instructions for using a pregnancy test, and I bought one for you to use." She paused and then looked Middy directly in her eyes and said, "I want you to try it, all you have to do is pee in it and then we'll know for sure." She waited and continued to lock eyes with Middy.

Middy reached for the instructions and read the first

few words and then said, "I know you have read all of this, so okay, I'll try it. Can I do it now?"

Patsy was relieved as she smiled and said, "yes and you can use my bathroom. The test kit is on the counter in my bathroom." She then explained how to use the test kit.

Middy stood and walked toward the door and then turned and said, "Okay, no peeking. I'll be back in a minute or two.

Patsy sat at the dining room table and said a silent prayer, asking God to spare Middy the embarrassment and pain of being pregnant.

Just after Patsy finished her prayer, Middy walked in with the test kit in her hand. She sat across from Patsy and held it in her hand and said, "What do you think?"

Patsy said, "I don't know what to think, but I did say a prayer for you, for us."

"I knew you would, thank you."

It took just a few minutes but seemed like much longer. It was negative. They both were relieved but knew this may not be exact as they smiled at each other and then stood up and embraced for a long moment.

They spent a quiet day together and relaxed. Patsy did some reading and Middy watched a movie on TV and took a nap. They had a late lunch and Patsy made some phone calls to Middy's agent and discussed some of the proposed upcoming events. She had advised them earlier that it might be another month or so before Middy would be ready to return. She wasn't ready to make any commitments at that point. They were both in bed earlier than usual and both felt better about the pregnancy test results.

Patsy had a hard time getting awake as she heard the

knocking on her bedroom door. She looked at her bedside clock, three o'clock. Then, she heard Middy's voice. She sat up and almost fell as she rushed to the door. She opened the door and saw Middy, looking happy and crying at the same time. Patsy wiped her sleepy eyes and said, "What is it? Are you okay?"

Middy hugged Patsy and said, "No, I'm not just okay, I'm great and I love you."

Patsy had no idea what was happing as Middy continued to hold her and cry. "What is it, Middy?"

She whispered in Patsy's ear. "I got my period all over the bed and I'm a mess, but I couldn't wait to tell you."

They finally stood back and Patsy said, "Thank the Lord."

She followed Middy upstairs and waited at her small kitchen table as Middy went to her bathroom to clean up. She made a pot of coffee and waited for Middy. This was great news and hopefully would get Middy back to a normal life again. Only time would tell.

C H A P T E R

Middy had not sung or even had any desire to sing. Now, after her talk with Patsy and actually feeling better about all that had happened to her, maybe, just maybe, it was time to think about getting back to doing what she felt like she was born to do…sing.

They had both rested most of the day after Middy's early awaking and confirming that she was not pregnant. Patsy was still sleeping and Middy quietly went downstairs and closed the door to the dining room and picked up one of her many guitars, this one was leaning in the corner of the room. She sat down at one of the dining room chairs and made a few chords and loved hearing the sound, a sound she had loved since she was five years old. Then, the big surprise. After making these pretty chords, she opened her mouth to sing one of her favorite songs and could not believe what she was hearing. Her voice was off key and very flat, nothing like her beautiful voice that had made her one of the most loved and respected singers in recent years. She stopped abruptly and closed her eyes and then cleared her throat. She then made a C chord on the guitar and very softly hummed, hoping to match the key of C. It wasn't just a note off, it was totally flat, like someone who is tone deaf.

She had known people like this, they could not hear that they were off key, but she always could and now she sounded like those tone-deaf people.

Middy stood, took the guitar and placed it back in the corner of the room and stared at it, like it was its fault. She was horrified. She had regained all of her abilities to talk, understand and communicate with no problems at all. Had this brain damage caused her to lose her ability to sing? She sat back down and cried, not realizing how loud she was crying as she said between sobs, "What's happening? Oh God, please don't let this happen to me."

Patsy had been awakened by her crying and loud talking. She got up and ran to the dining room and saw Middy sitting in a chair with a look of horror on her face. She could not remember Middy looking so distraught and confused. She was waving her arms and continuing to cry and ask why this was happening to her. Patsy went to her and knelt down in front of her and looked up into her teary eyes.

"Middy, honey, what in the world is wrong? Are you hurting, are you having pain?"

Middy glared at Patsy and said in a choked voice, "Yes, I'm hurting, I'm hurting in my heart. My life may be over, Patsy."

Patsy's first thought was a heart attack and panicked. "Oh, Middy, please stay calm. Maybe it's just indigestion or heart burn. I'll call 911, please try to calm down and relax. You know I'll take care of you, honey."

Middy stood and screamed at Patsy, saying, "It's not a heart attack, damn it. I'm not sick...don't call anyone. It's my voice, Patsy, I can't sing, I can't sing. What am I going to do?" She was shaking as she spoke.

Patsy was so relieved that it wasn't her heart or anything threating her life. She knew Middy had not sung since the attack and felt sure she just needed some time to get back to her normal life. She wanted to help her, but at that moment had no idea what to do or who she should call.

Patsy waited as Middy began to calm down and then she smiled at Patsy and said, "I'm sorry for being so crazy. This is such a shock to me."

They stood and looked into each other's eyes, both hoping and praying that this would pass, but neither knew if it would, for sure.

Patsy finally broke the silence and said, "Middy, I'm not sure who can help us with this problem, but I really feel it must be from the stress you have had over the past weeks. You are fine in every other way and I don't think it had anything to do with your head injury or surgery."

Middy frowned and said, "You mean, brain injury, right."

Patsy knew this was not the right time to reason with her and took her in her arms as she always did when Middy was upset. They embraced for a long time and Patsy said, "I want to suggest something and hope you will, at least consider it."

They stood back holding hands as they always did and Middy said, "You know I'll listen, Patsy. You are the most important person in my life."

Patsy smiled and said, "That is so sweet, you know we both feel the same about each other. Now, there are other people that are very important in your life and I think they can be very helpful in getting you through this."

"Other people?" Middy was frowning now.

"Yes Middy, two others, your mom and dad."

Middy was silent and continued to frown at Patsy. "Just what do you think they can do? I know they love me and I love them, but they're not doctors."

Patsy smiled and placed her hand on Middy's shoulder and said, "No, they're not doctors, but they have a special connection with you that no one else has. I think their love and support is what you need now." She hesitated and then said, "Please allow me to call them, it can't hurt and I really believe they can help you more than anyone."

Middy cried again and said, "Patsy Holt, you always have suggestions and ideas that I never think of. I will agree, but I want to make the call."

Patsy again smiled with tears in her eyes, so thankful that Middy had agreed. She also knew her confession with Tim and Mary still had to happen. It would have to wait now until Middy got through this.

CHAPTER

Middy went upstairs and Patsy was sure she must be making that phone call to her parents. After about thirty minutes, she came back downstairs and found Patsy still in the dining room. They both smiled at each other and Middy said, "Well, mom said to tell you hello and that she loves you." She continued to smile and the continued with, "and thanks to you for this suggestion, it is even better."

Patsy couldn't wait for her to continue. "Better, how could it be better? They are coming, aren't they?" she said as she frowned at Middy.

Middy laughed aloud for one of the few times since her injury. "No Patsy, they're not coming."

"And that's better? Middy Adams, you are playing with me now. I know when you are kidding, now what's going on?"

"We're going there; we're going to Jackson and spend the weekend with mom and dad. That's what's better. I'm so excited and happy to be going home for a visit and of course with you, Patsy Holt."

Patsy was thinking what a change in Middy's attitude;

she was actually laughing and seemed happier than she had seen her in weeks. This was a great idea!

Middy and Patsy arrived at Tim and Mary's home on Friday afternoon. Patsy had driven as she always did when they traveled by car. Tim and Mary were so excited to have their two favorite ladies for a weekend visit. They had no idea why they had asked to spend some time with them but were looking forward to a happy time.

Mary had made dinner and her famous chocolate cream pie for dessert. It was one of Middy's favorite desserts and Patsy had had it for the first time after meeting Middy over six years ago and liked it also.

The dinner was great and as they all enjoyed a piece of the famous pie, then the conversation changed to Middy's recovery as Mary said, "Well honey, have you thought about when you will return to work, I mean tour."

Everyone laughed and Middy said, "Well, it is work, Mom, but I don't have to tell you, I love it." She sat her fork down and looked at Patsy with a slight frown.

Mary never missed anything with her "angel" and immediately noticed her frown as said, "Honey, did I say something to upset you? You look so sad."

Middy again looked at Patsy and then back at her mom and said, "Oh Mom, you never fail to notice every expression I make."

"Well, are you okay? I know you wanted all four of us to have some time together."

Middy wasn't ready to broach the subject about her voice, but her mom had given her little choice. "Mom, I do, or I should say, we do want to talk about something, but first of all, I'm okay. I have, for the most part, returned to my old self." She smiled and waited for her mom's response.

And her response was immediate. "You said for the most part, so there must be some other part that is not just right."

Middy looked again at Patsy and said, "Well, we wanted to wait until tomorrow, but it's okay." She paused and looked at her mom, then her dad and said, "Can we sit in the living room?"

Patsy helped Mary clear the table and Middy went to the bathroom. Mary was continuing to frown as she looked at Patsy and said, "Oh, Patsy, please tell me there's nothing bad wrong."

Patsy was not surprised as Mary was a constant worrier about Middy, and with all Middy had been through lately, she was more paranoid than ever. "Mary, please don't be upset, this is not anything we can't handle. She just needs our love and support now more than ever."

"And you're not going to tell what this is about?"

Patsy smiled and said, "No, this is Middy's issue and she wants to share her concern with you and Tim, so please let her have this special time."

Middy returned to the kitchen and said, "Well, looks like I waited long enough to let you two clean up." They all laughed and Mary seemed more relaxed.

It was time, and Middy knew the suspense was getting to her mom. "Mom, is it okay if we have a glass of wine as we talk?"

Tim and Mary seldom drank alcohol, but did keep wine for guest and special occasions, and this was one. "Sure, honey you know where we keep it, if you would like to do the honors. I will have a glass, but not sure if you dad will. You can ask him."

Patsy went with Middy and found the wine in a bottom kitchen cabinet, behind several canned goods. They smiled at each other as Patsy got down on all fours and took out a bottle of red and one white wine. They were not chilled, but would be okay. They took both bottles to the living room with four glasses and set them on the coffee table.

Tim had just returned from the bathroom and frowned as he saw the wine setting on the coffee table. Middy just smiled at her dad and said, "I guess you don't care for a glass, right Dad."

He did manage to smile and said, "No, thanks. I am still full from the dinner your mom made."

Patsy opened both bottles and poured a half glass of red wine and handed it to Mary. She then filled a glass for Middy and then poured a full glass of white for herself. Now was the time, and Middy was ready.

After taking a gulp of wine, Middy smiled and said, "Well, I know I've kept you all in suspense and I'm sorry to do you like this." She paused and took another swallow and the said, "It's my voice that has me so upset."

Mary was quick to respond. "Your voice...what do you mean?"

"I can't sing." She stared at her mom and then her dad.

They both were silent as they waited for her to continue. And she did continue as she started to cry. "I'm tone deaf, I can't carry a tune. I think I may have brain damage." She covered her face with both hands and sobbed.

Mary wanted to comfort her, but continued to remain

seated as she said, "Honey, there's nothing wrong with you brain. It must just be from the stress you've been under."

Middy looked at her mom with tears flowing and said, "That's what Patsy has said, I'm so glad to know you think the same." She looked at her dad and then. "Dad, do you think it could be the stress also?"

Tim did not hesitate as he smiled and said, "Honey, I totally agree with your mom and Patsy. I think you just need some time to get through this."

Middy did feel more relieved hearing her parents agree with Patsy. It meant so much to have their involvement with her. She needed this support and love and the three people she loved most, were sitting with her at this moment.

After a long moment of silence, Tim said, "Honey, as we have all agreed, this should go away with time, but there are other means of help."

Middy frowned. "Other means?"

"Yes, I'm no expert, but there is speech therapy, and other counseling possibilities you might consider."

Mary then felt it was her time to lend more support as she said, "Your dad is right, this could be an option for you, but I feel like time will be the key to you getting your voice back. You know we believe in your abilities and are so proud of you." Mary hesitated and then looked at Patsy and said, "You have someone so special in your life, someone few people have. Patsy has been your strongest support and you both share a love that is very special. We know she will always be there for you as she has in the past."

Patsy was staring at Mary as she made these comments and suddenly stood up and said, "Please excuse me, I'm not feeling well." She covered her mouth with her hand and ran down the hall to the guest bathroom.

Mary looked shocked and said, "Do you need to help her, Middy?"

Middy didn't answer her mom, but instead took another gulp of her wine. She knew why Patsy was upset and wanted her parents to know why also, but it wasn't her place to tell them. She knew Patsy Holt had to tell them why she had left her, and the reason she was not with her when she was attacked.

Mary couldn't wait and finally walked to the guest bathroom and knocked gently and said, "Patsy, are you, all right?"

Patsy moaned and said, "I feel sick, just let me have a few minutes."

Mary couldn't imagine why she had suddenly fallen sick. She seemed fine until she began to praise her for her loyalty and love for Middy. Then she thought of the times in the hospital when Patsy had left the room or made excuses to leave after they had praised her for her love and protection for Middy. Then the big question, the question she and Tim had wondered about. They both had heard Patsy say that she would never leave Middy again. The word again had remained in their thoughts. They had not asked if she was with Middy when she was attacked. Mary walked back to the living room and sat across from Middy and frowned.

Middy could see that her mom had questions and she thought she knew they must be about Patsy. She did not speak but tried be prepared to answer her mom's concerns.

Mary cleared her throat and looked at Tim and then

back at Middy. "Middy, you know you do not have to answer questions that you feel are none of our business, but this is concerning to us." She again looked at Tim. He had closed his eyes, making no sound. Mary continued. "We have had questions about Patsy that we have not asked, but now, I feel that we should be allowed to ask." She looked at Middy and continued to frown.

Middy reached for the bottle of wine and filled her empty glass. After setting down the bottle she said, "Well, I'm sure your main concern is about Patsy not being with me when I was attacked."

Mary looked surprised. "Are you saying she was not with you...where was she?"

"I had hoped and wanted Patsy to tell you all about this, but as you can see, she is to upset to discuss it." She then took another gulp of wine and closed her eyes. She opened her eyes and continued. "So, I am going to save Patsy the agony of talking about this. I know what I'm going to tell you will not be acceptable to you and dad." She noticed her dad's eyes not only open but bulging and looking at her. She wished the wine would relax her, but she was totally stressed with having to talk about the person she loved most in her life being a lesbian.

All three were surprised as they saw Patsy walking back into the living room. She went directly and sat next to Middy and took the bottle of white wine and refilled her glass. She looked at Mary and then Tim and said, "I heard the last few things you said about me and do not want to cause Middy anymore stress, trying to explain my actions."

Middy placed her hand on Patsy's arm and said, "Patsy, you've been sick, I can tell them. It's okay."

Patsy glared at Middy and said, "Middy, we both have known that this moment would come and we also know that it is my responsibility to tell your parents."

Middy knew Patsy wanted to do this and hoped she could get through it, but most of all she hoped and prayed that her parents would accept her for who she is, and not judge her.

Patsy was shaking as she took a large drink from her glass of wine. She sat down the glass and looked at her best friend's mom and dad, thinking how they must feel about gay people. She laced her fingers and then said, "I don't have to tell you how much Middy means to me. You both know the love we have is very special, as you just said a few minutes ago, Mary." She turned to look at Middy and then continued. "I had kept a secret from Middy and the rest of the world, including my parents and my brother until a few months ago, and now I want you both to know the truth about me."

Tim and Mary were solemn as they sat in complete silence, glaring at Patsy and waiting for the big secret. Middy had her head bowed with her eyes closed.

Patsy knew it was best to get this out in the open and blurted it out. "Tim and Mary, I'm a gay person." She stared at each one of them and waited for their reaction, but there was none, only silence.

Middy raised her head and opened her eyes, looking at Tim and Mary. They had no expression and seemed to be waiting for Patsy to continue. Mary finally said, "Well, that is really none of our business about your sexual orientation. My question is where you were when Middy needed you the most."

Patsy felt relieved that that they seemed to accept her being gay, but now must explain about her relationship with Agnes Barnes. She again looked at Middy for her support and said, "I must tell them about Agnes, do you agree?"

Middy smiled at her and said, "Patsy, we need to tell it all, but most of all, we are together now, forever."

It took Patsy several minutes to explain how she had told Middy about being gay and then asking for time off to hopefully clear her mind. She told them about calling Agnes Barnes, an old classmate from her high school days and then taking her to meet Middy.

Tim and Mary listened without comment until Patsy told them about moving to Nashville with Agnes and leaving Middy alone.

Mary spoke first saying, "So, you just left Middy to be with your lover and had no concern for Middy's safety, is that what you are telling us, Patsy?"

Patsy knew this would be impossible for them to accept. Tim and Mary had always believed that Patsy would be with Middy, no matter what happened. Patsy was silent for a long moment and then said, "I really need to tell you how all of this happened. Please let me finish before you pass judgement."

Mary nodded and Tim frowned and said, "Okay, Patsy…we're listening."

Patsy again looked into Middy's eyes for support and felt her love and support. "Middy was very unhappy with my arrangement with Agnes and actually asked us to move out. I really wanted to stay but did understand how upsetting this was for Middy. We moved to a condo in Nashville and one night, I called Middy's number by mistake and we spoke for a brief moment and then her phone went dead." Patsy stopped and cried as all three waited for her to continue. "She had been attacked then and I went to check on her and called the paramedics, and you know the rest of the story."

Tim stood up and looked down at Patsy and said in a gruff voice, "So, this guy, this Skaggs guy, he attacked Middy and rap..." He could not use the word rape as he choked up and sat back down. "My next question is about your...friend, or whatever. She was the one to influence Skaggs and then got off because of lack of evidence, right?"

Middy had listened without comment, but now felt she should defend Patsy. "Mom, Dad, I would like to take it from here, so again, like Patsy said, let me finish." She looked at the wine bottle and decided she had had enough and didn't really need false courage at this point. "Agnes Barnes never liked me and thought of me as a threat to Patsy and her. We are sure she encouraged Jimmy Skaggs to attack me, but that is over now and he is dead, and Agnes is out of the picture. Patsy and I have reconciled this and both agree that we will spend the rest of our lives together. She has committed herself to me and God and I believe her. We are not sexually involved and never have been or never will be, but we do love each other." She looked at Patsy then. "We are both fine now and need your understanding and love. I am not asking either of you to forgive her or me. That will be between you and God. She closed her eyes again and bowed her head.

Mary stood and went to Middy and Patsy then and asked them to make room for her on the couch. She sat between them and put an arm around each one. They all three cried for a few moments and then Mary said, "I want you both to know that this subject will not be discussed by us again, but most of all Tim and I want both of you to know that we are happy and thankful that you are back together like you were meant to be. We are all blessed and thank the Lord for bringing us to this moment."

THE END

EPILOGUE

It has now been two years since Middy and Patsy made that trip to Tim and Mary's home. It had been the end of a tragic time for all four of them, but also new beginnings. Middy had taken the advice from her parents and Patsy. Relaxing and accepting her many blessings, her beautiful voice had returned and she began to sing again. They had been back on tour and Middy had released another album entitled, "The Blessings of Life." It had gone to number one. She wrote most of the songs on the album and also included several spirituals that she knew would continue to inspire her for the rest of her life. The trauma she had experienced had truly made her stronger. She would always remember the people who had touched her life during her recovery with their love, kindness and support. She and Patsy had put the past behind them and were thankful for each day they had and continued to thank God for allowing them this special love and their Total Commitment to each other. Patsy had memories of Agnes Barnes, but no desire to ever see her again.

Rick and Kathy Stone had a little girl now, just one year old. She was named after her Godmother and Middy was so proud, they had given her that honor and Rick and Kathy knew "Little Middy" would always be as proud of her name as they were.

Agnes Barnes had returned to Austin, Texas and opened her own animal rescue clinic. She worked closely with the veterinarian she had worked for in the past and loved being back home and helping small animals. She thought about Patsy less often, but most of all regretted her involvement in Middy's attack. She knew she could have spent many years in prison and thanked God that she was free. She would always pray each night and ask God to forgive her, not only for the trauma she had caused Middy, her family and Patsy but also her control of a young man that led to his death.

Beth Hatcher was still with Vanderbilt Medical Center and continued to enjoy helping people with health concerns. She thought about Middy many times when she was alone and during quiet times. She would always remember Middy asking her to work for her and be her assistant, but knew nursing was what she wanted. She did feel a special closeness to Middy that she never understood. It was like she had a connection, like family. She thought it must just be a feeling that you develop with someone as kind and loving as Middy. Only Middy and Patsy would know the truth.

Tim and Mary attended many of Middy's concerts and always had front row seats. They held hands and sang along with their "special angel" as she closed each show with her signature song, "The Shoebox."